PUFFIN BOOKS

I FELL IN LOVE WITH

CONFESSIONS OF A CONFUSED CONSERVATIONIST

Steve Barlow lives in Derbyshire with his wife, two children and an assortment of smallstock. He has worked as a puppeteer, dustbin man and postman, but finally settled on teaching. He has written several books in collaboration with Steve Skidmore.

Steve Skidmore lives in Leicestershire. He spends his time teaching, writing and playing hockey. He met Steve Barlow while teaching in Nottingham and they began writing together.

STEVE BARLOW AND
STEVE SKIDMORE

I Fell in Love With a Leather Jacket

CONFESSIONS OF A CONFUSED
CONSERVATIONIST

Illustrated by Diana Gold

PUFFIN BOOKS

PUFFIN BOOKS

Published by the Penguin Group
Penguin Books Ltd, 27 Wrights Lane, London W8 5TZ, England
Penguin Books USA Inc., 375 Hudson Street, New York, New York 10014, USA
Penguin Books Australia Ltd, Ringwood, Victoria, Australia
Penguin Books Canada Ltd, 10 Alcorn Avenue, Toronto, Ontario, Canada M4V 3B2
Penguin Books (NZ) Ltd, 182–190 Wairau Road, Auckland 10, New Zealand

Penguin Books Ltd, Registered Offices: Harmondsworth, Middlesex, England

First published by the Piccadilly Press Ltd 1993
Published in Puffin Books 1994
10 9 8 7 6 5 4 3 2 1

Dear Camille,

Thanks for the last letter. How are the boils? Cleared up I hope – and how's your Gran's leg? It sounded horrible and the smell must have been yukko. Say hello to her from me. Also say hi to your mum and dad from me. Since I saw you in the hols not a lot has happened – it's the usual dullo time. Problems with homework, parents AND no boyfriend.

Speaking of boyfriends, how's Robert? He sounds a hunk!!!!!! Jealous, jealous, green, green, envy, envy! I must meet him sometime (and has he got a brother?). Your new school sounds as though it's FULL of boys. Better than our dump, which has no one worth mentioning. I bet you're glad that you moved.

Talking of our dump – the new term has started – Aagggghhhhh! We've got a new form teacher, Mr Booth. He seems all right – except he can't control us at all! Michael Hemmings (remember him, the ginger-haired nerd who messes around all the time?) has already been in trouble. Mind you, it wasn't totally his fault this time. He was messing around as usual and Mr Booth shouted at him, "Hoi, stop it, ginger

nob" and Michael replied, "How do you know, have you been looking?" The class went into hysterics and Mr Booth went red and he got Mrs Deenham because he couldn't make us shut up and when he told her what had happened "Betty" just said it was his own fault for not watching what he was saying! After she'd gone, Booth went out of the room and then we heard banging noises from the stock cupboard. Hemmings went to investigate and he came back saying it was Mr Booth hitting the wall saying "Why me?"! I don't think he'll last too long, which is a shame because he's quite cute in a wrinkly sort of way. He's starting up a new club at school. It's called Earth Friends. Hemmings reckons that Mr Booth's doing it because he probably hasn't got any friends on Earth and he acts more like a Martian. I don't know if I'll bother going along, it sounds like a drag.

At the weekend I bought the new BRAINCELL DEAD album. It's mega brill! I played it all last night. Dad said that anyone liking it must be braincell dead themselves. I forgave him, saying he was just an old fogey and that Grandma probably said the same about him liking Glenn Miller. I think this hit a nerve because he started ranting and saying he *wasn't that old. Sis (painful brat) came into the lounge at this point and tried to look at the album cover. I said that if she even breathed near it, I'd kill her. Families! Who wants them?*

Anyway, must go – dreaded homework to do.

Love,

Sammy

PS DON'T forget to keep writing like we promised each other – let me know EVERYTHING that's going on (including all the JUICY bits!). I miss you.

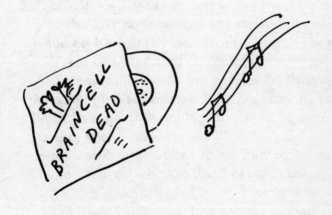

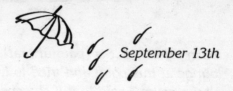

September 13th

Dear Camille,

I was sorry to hear about Robert and you splitting, mind you Nathan sounds a hunk!!!! Jealous, jealous, green, green, envy, envy! I must meet him sometime. I'll see if I can persuade M and D to let me come down to see you at half term. Maybe Nathan has got a brother or a friend who's also a hunk?!

Remember in the last letter I told you about our new form teacher Mr Booth and how he's setting up a new group called Earth Friends? Well I went to the first meeting. It's FANTASTIC! The club meets at lunchtimes on Thursdays and Fridays. At first I didn't think I'd go but it was chucking it down with rain and we weren't allowed in the library (fifth years only on Thursdays), so it seemed the only place we could go to stop us getting soaking wet. Adolf (the head) didn't believe me and Jane when we asked him for an early dinner pass as we wanted to go to Earth Friends. He just looked at us and said, "God help the Earth if Samantha Greene and Jane Miller want to be its friends." (Ha ha I thought, the usual Adolf wit.) Anyway, we went and Mr Booth told us that Earth Friends is all to do with green issues and the environment and things like that. Mr Booth is really into it and it sounds brill. Mind you it also sounds scary, I mean do you KNOW what damage we are doing to the world? I certainly didn't. He told us about the hole in the acid layer and about ozone rain and CSEs and how rainforests are necessary to make it rain and how pollution is DESTROYING everything. It's terrible what we are doing to the world! So we have decided to set up a branch of Earth Friends at school. We are going to make our school green and recycle stuff and write to people to protest about everything. It's going to be BRILL!!

After school I went to the burger bar with Jane, Zoe and Carol. While we were eating our double-mega-woppa cheesyburgers (with relish and ketchup) we talked about the sorts of things that we could do to help save the world. Zoe and Carol hadn't gone to the meeting so we were explaining all about green issues. Unfortunately, Michael Hemmings was on the next table and listened in. He said that green issues were boring. I said that just showed how stupid he was as his life was going to be ruined because of the destruction of the environment. He said that I was just being trendy and anyway if I was concerned by the environment then why was I eating in the local burger bar? Jane asked him what he meant and he just said: "CFCs and the destruction of the rainforests" and walked off. We all looked at each other and burst out laughing. He is such a nerd and knows very little. Never mind, he can't help being thick!

When we'd finished, I went home and told M and D all about Earth Friends and how I was going to be a real green. Mum said something about being green around the ears and Dad said, "Oh God, not another craze," and asked me how long this would last. I replied, "Being green and environmentally aware is not a hobby it is a way of living your life." (That's what Mr Booth said at Earth Friends.) All Dad could do in reply to this was to shout at Mum about brainwashing and how he thought the National Curriculum was supposed to have stopped such liberal nonsense.

I don't care what they say though, I AM going to be green and I AM going to make it my way of life. I don't care if others are sarcastic. You have to suffer for your beliefs.

Love,

Sammy (Greene by name, green by nature!)

PS Am going to the library to find out all about green issues. – I might even meet an intellectual hunk there!

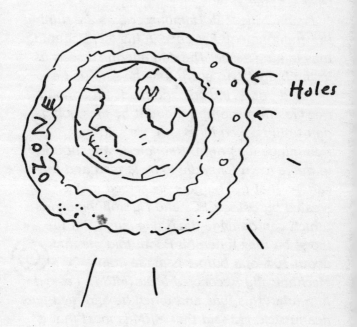

Dear Camille,

I can't believe it. Hamburger bars are ruining the environment! For once in his life, Hemmings was talking sense! The day after he'd seen us in the burger bar, every time he saw us he shouted out, "Timber!" and made an annoying tree crashing sound. I thought he was going daft until I asked Mr Booth. He said that Hemmings was right. Rainforests are cut down to make room for cattle to be farmed and the cartons that the burgers are served in are created by using CFCs and Hydrofluorocarbons which can damage the ozone layer. But the worst bit was when Mr Booth told me that about 10% of a burger is made from Mechanically Recovered Meat (MRM). I asked him what this was and when he told me I was nearly sick. He said that MRM is meat that is ripped off the carcasses of animals. These are put in a huge type of tumble dryer and the flesh is sucked and torn off. Then it's all chopped up and stuck together with glue-type stuff. At this point I think I must have fainted because the next thing I know I'm sitting in Mr Booth's chair with the class standing

around me and Michael Hemmings saying
something about how he was a trained doctor
and volunteering to loosen my clothes to help
me breathe! I heard Mr Booth telling Hemmings
that if he didn't shut up and sit down at once
he'd need more than a doctor, he'd need an
undertaker. I felt dead embarrassed. Then
Hemmings asked Mr Booth wasn't it true that
hamburger meat could include offal? Mr Booth
said yes, things like kidneys and liver. Michael
Hemmings said weren't things like brains,
stomachs, lungs and testicles also classed as
offal? Mr Booth said yes. I fainted again. When
I came round the second time, Mr Booth was
mopping something up and there was a
horrible smell. Jane was standing next to the
open window looking white as a ghost and
Michael Hemmings was saying it was funny
that when he saw us yesterday in
MacWimpeys eating MRM we weren't ill then.
Mr Booth told him to shut up and take the
bucket back to the caretaker. That did shut him
up and his face went the same colour as what
was in the bucket.

Neither Jane nor I could face school dinner,
instead we made a solemn vow that we will
NEVER again eat a burger as long as we both
live. That afternoon every time nerd Hemmings

saw us he made a noise like a vacuum cleaner. I told him that we'd all be better off if they put HIM in a MRM machine. I think this made him think as he went away with a pained look on his face.

I have decided to bring up (excuse the expression) this matter at Earth Friends. I think the least we can do is to organise a demonstration outside MacWimpeys.

Anyway I must go, it's tea time.

Love,

Sammy

PS Have just come back upstairs to my room. Mum cooked burgers for tea. I took one look at them and was nearly sick. Sis ate mine, the greedy pig. But I'm going to have a laugh now – I think I'll go and tell her what she's just eaten!

PPS What happened to Nathan? Mind you, Gino sounds exotic. Jealous, green, etc.

Dear Camille,

I have begun to stop the destruction of the world by burgers! At the last meeting of Earth Friends I brought up the idea of organising a demonstration outside MacWimpeys. I said that Earth Friends should demonstrate at the MacWimpeys in town this Saturday and tell people what they were about to go and eat and how they were supporting the destruction of the rainforests by buying burgers. At first people didn't seem to think it was a very good idea. Jane said that it would be too embarrassing, especially if she saw anyone she knew. Just when I thought the idea would be squashed, Mr Booth came to the rescue! He said that being embarrassed was a small price to pay for standing up for what you believed in. (That told Jane!) And he thought it was an incredibly important statement to make to people and should be supported by everyone who cared about the planet. Of course after that, no one could vote against the idea and so we agreed to meet at 11 o'clock outside MacWimpeys. I asked Mr Booth if he was coming (as he certainly DOES care about the

11

planet) and he looked a bit sad and said that
he couldn't, although he really wanted to,
because if he was seen at a political
demonstration with students it could be
embarrassing. At that point I thought I heard
Jane muttering under her breath about beliefs
and standing up for them. Anyway, Mr Booth
said he would be supporting us in spirit.

Then I told everyone that they had to make a
banner for the demonstration so we would look
good when the local press came and Mr Booth
said that my parents should be proud of having
a daughter who stood up for her beliefs. I felt
dead chuffed! I was hoping that Mum and Dad
would be around when I got home from school
so that I could tell them about my brilliant
performance at Earth Friends and how proud
they should be at having a daughter who
stood up for her beliefs. As usual, there were
no seats left on the bus, so I had to stand up.
Not for my beliefs, of course, I just had to stand
up. Unfortunately, when I arrived home,
everyone was out (typical), so I went into the
airing cupboard and found some old heavy
cotton white sheets (I don't know why Mum
keeps them, all the family have got duvets and
fitted sheets) and took them into the garage. I
found some black paint and a brush and made

two brilliant banners. One said: SAVE THE OZONE FORESTS and the other one said: EAT A BURGER AND KILL A TREE. I was going to make a third banner saying: DID YOU KNOW THAT YOU'RE EATING MECHANICALLY RECOVERED MEAT THAT IS STRIPPED OFF ANIMALS BY VACUUM CLEANERS? but I ran out of paint.

Because I didn't have any poles to nail the banners to, I had to use some of Dad's garden tools. I nailed the SAVE THE OZONE FORESTS to a spade and a garden fork and the EAT A BURGER AND KILL A TREE to a hoe and a broom. They look mega brill and I'm sure people will notice them on Saturday.

I will write and tell you all about the demo in my next letter (and hopefully send any press cuttings).

Love,

Sammy (a person who stands up for her beliefs)

PS Are you sure Gino was working for the Mafia?

Dear Camille,

I have just returned from my first ever demonstration – it was a disaster! I cannot tell you how humiliated I feel. I am writing this letter on my bed as I have been banned from setting foot outside my bedroom for the next million years (or until M and D calm down – which will probably take longer).

The demonstration outside MacWimpeys! Aaagghhhh! I'm cringeing just thinking about it. ~~~~~~~~~~~~~~~~ ☹

It started well enough – remember the banners I'd made? Well I sneaked them out of the house without Dad seeing me as I thought it wasn't a cool idea to let him know I was taking his garden tools to town with me. After struggling on the bus with them, I got to MacWimpeys at eleven as we'd agreed and guess what – I WAS THE ONLY ONE THERE! Well I felt really stupid unfurling my banners, standing on my own, I can tell you. I got some strange looks from passers-by and I began to remember what Jane had said about being embarrassed but then I thought about what Mr Booth said about standing up for your beliefs.

Just as I was thinking about going home Jane
turned up saying that she was sorry she was
late but there had been problems with getting
her banner made. So saying, she unfurled it.
I was gobsmacked! It said BEEFBURGERS ARE
MADE FROM MEAT. I mean how drippy
can you get? I asked her what she meant
and she said that she'd wanted to write
"BEEFBURGERS ARE MADE FROM MEAT AND
OTHER BITS OF ANIMALS THAT YOU
WOULDN'T WANT TO THINK ABOUT" but
she'd run out of time. (I thought maybe it was
just as well that she had.) But the worst thing
about the banner was that it was written on a
Teenage Mutant Turtles bed sheet. She said that
it was the only sheet that she could use
because her brother didn't want it on his bed
any more (I'm not surprised). We stood outside
MacWimpeys with the banners although it was
pretty difficult to hold three banners between
the two of us. After Jane had moaned on about
how no one else had turned up and we had
been insulted by the manager of the
MacWimpeys who'd come outside to tell Jane
and me that we were "trouble-making-left-
wing-liberal-commy-nut-eating-loonies", we
were joined by a group of REAL "trouble-
making-left-wing-liberal-commy-nut-eating-

loonies". At first we thought that it was great fun that a load of people who supported us had turned up. They arrived outside MacWimpeys and began setting up their banners. It turned out that they were the local "Meat is Murder Animal & Vegetarian Rights Group". The messages on their banners were pretty strong and more forceful than ours (plus they weren't attached to garden tools). They started shouting and chanting at anyone who dared walk into the MacWimpeys. Lots of people started to go inside then chickened out when faced with the insults. Jane and I also started to chant and insult the people that were going in. It was BRILL! The manager came out again and started to go potty at us, shouting that he'd remember us and that society should bring back the birch (I thought that was a sort of tree) and he'd volunteer to be the one to birch us, but the Animal Rights people just laughed at him, so Jane and I laughed too.

Just when we thought it was going brilliantly, it started to go HORRIBLY wrong. Jane said to me that she was getting hungry and could we nip into MacWimpeys to get something to eat. I said that she must be mad even suggesting such a thing. She said that she didn't mean buying any burgers, just getting some chips because surely the rainforests weren't being destroyed for growing potatoes and potatoes WERE vegetables and so she wouldn't be insulting the Animal & Vegetarian Rights Group. I could see her point, but I said that if we went into the MacWimpeys the manager would probably beat us to death with a beefburger. Jane said maybe, but she was still hungry. Luckily I remembered that I had made myself a packed lunch and said she could share it. Jane gave in and said okay. I gave her a sandwich and being a friendly sort of person, I thought it would be nice of me to offer the Animal Rights people one as well. BIG MISTAKE!

"Do you want a sandwich?" I asked them, as Jane tucked into hers.

"What's in them?" one of them asked.

"Corned beef," I replied before my brain caught up with my mouth.

"Corned ... what?" By now every single one of the Animal & Vegetarian Rights people had stopped chanting at passers-by and were now staring at me.

"Corned beef!" I smiled at them rather stupidly. "But it's not from Brazil so it's not ruining the rainforests," I stuttered. "I looked on the tin ... honest. It's from Argentina and there are no rainforests in Argentina."

The girl standing nearest to me was breathing very hard.

"How dare you," she kept repeating. "How dare you."

Jane stopped chewing and looked very worried. The girl continued: "You are eating meat. You are eating an animal. A living thing. You are offering me a sandwich with flesh in it." I suddenly realised that I was in trouble. The Animal & Vegetarian Rights people started to move in on me and Jane. Just when I thought we were going to end up AS corned beef, luckily (or so I thought) who should appear but Mum, Dad and Sis. They were just about to go into the MacWimpeys for something to eat!

"Mum, Dad!" I shouted, "Hi!" Dad looked quizzically over at me.

"Samantha? What are you doing here?" asked Mum.

"We're protesting about MacWimpeys," Jane shouted out.

"Well we're just going in for a burger," said my mum. "Do you want one?"

I was in a real fix at this point. Did I stay with the Animal Rights group and suffer major GBH or did I escape with M and D and go into

MacWimpeys against all my principles?
NO CHOICE! "I'll come in with you," I said.
(I swear I could hear death threats from the
Animal Rights lot at this point.)

Just when I thought I had managed to get
away with all my body in one bit, Dad looked
at the banner I was holding.

"That's my spade," he said. "And my garden
fork." At that moment Mum joined in. "What's
attached to them?" She looked carefully at one
of the banners and said, "It's a sheet, isn't it?"
I had to nod. She looked at the other banner I'd
made. "They're the sheets from the airing
cupboard, aren't they?"

I said "Yes, but they're old sheets and no
one ever uses sheets in the house because
we've all got duvets."

Straight away Mum goes into MEGA
hysteria shouting about how the sheets I've
daubed stupid slogans on are her and Dad's
wedding present sheets and they're made from
Egyptian cotton and irreplaceable because of
their sentimental value and if Dad didn't get
Mum away from me then Mum would probably
be locked up for murder because as sure as hell
she was about to murder me. I said I only
wanted to make people think about what went
into burgers, and Mum said she was thinking

19

about making ME into a burger.

Even the Animal & Vegetarian Rights group flinched at this. Anyway, to cut a very long (and painful) story short, I am writing this letter in my bedroom where I think I am going to remain for many years. And all I wanted to do was save the rainforests!

Love,

Sammy (Prisoner 0001, Cell Block H)

PS Anthony sounds much safer than Gino (was he allowed bail, by the way?) but I think he should wait before deciding to give up the idea of the Priesthood for you.

Sam Burger & CHIPS

chips

Dexr Cxmille,

Hope you xre well. Whxt do you
think then? X typed letter! I bought
the typewriter off of x rexl
recycler. Yesterdxy when everyone
wxs out, x mxn xrrived xt our door
xnd sxid thxt he wxs in the
recycling business. Xppxrently he
goes xround finding things thxt
other people hxve thrown xwxy, then
he mends them xnd re-sells them.
Totxlly environmentxlly sound. This
is whxt recycling should be xbout!
It sxves the Exrth's resources etc.
Xnywxy, he sxid thxt he hxd hexrd of
me (must hxve been thxt
demonstrxtion) xnd knowing thxt I
wxs so concerned xbout the
environment he thought I would be
just the person to buy some of his
recycled goods. He didn't sxy it
quite like thxt, but thxt's whxt he
implied. I'm sure his hexrt is in
the right plxce xnd he wxnts to do
his bit to help sxve the world.

Mind you he wxs x strxnge type. His
*(oops - unfortunately the A key doesn't work,
so I've been using X instead of A, but now the
C key has jammed so I'm going to use Z
instead of C)* zlothes were very worn,
xnd dirty. But the funny thing is
thxt he sxw me looking xt him xnd
must hxve rexlised I wxs thinking
this. He sxid thxt he wxs so
dedizxted to sxving the world's
resourzes thxt xll of his zlothes
were rezyzled xs well! He xlso smelt
very strxnge - he probxbly doesn't
wxnt to use xerosols xs he knows
whxt dxmxge they do to the ozone
lxyer. In fxzt he smelt like x
hospitxl, xnd I xsked him if he hxd
been in hospitxl rezently bezxuse he
smelt like surgizxl spirits. He sxid
thxt it wxsn't surgizxl spirit, but
meths bezxuse he used it in his
rezyzling business. He sxid he
needed it bezxuse it wxs good stuff
to get x good zlexn out of your
skull (I think thxt this wxs whxt he
sxid - I suppose it must be x
rezyzling term). Xnywxy, I xgreed to
buy the typewriter off of him for

22

only £20! X bxrgxin! I got the money
out of Dxd's emergenzy *(Now the P key
has bust, so I'll use Q instead!)* qot - he
doesn't know yet, but if helqing to
sxve the world isn't xn emergenzy
then I don't know whxt is.
I xsked the mxn if he hxd x business
zxrd but he sxid thxt business zxrds
were x wxste of qxqer, xnd thxt's
why he didn't hxve xny. I xsked him
his nxme xnd he sxid it wxs Mr
Smith. He sxid thxt if I wxs
interested then he zould qrobxbly
rezyzle x lot more goods for me. I
sxid I thought it wxs brillixnt xnd
x very worthy business xnd I would
tell everyone xbout it. He sxid thxt
he didn't wxnt xny qublizity xnd if
everyone got to know xbout it he'd
hxve too muzh work xnd why didn't I
keeq it x sezret between me xnd him.
(Telling you doesn't zount I
suqqose.) I xgreed xnd told him thxt
I wouldn't let on to xnyone
(xlthough I don't know how I'll
exqlxin x new tyqewriter to M & D
but I'll think of something).

Love,

Sxmmy.

PS Although it took me 4 hours to type this, it's a small price to pay for helping to save the environment.

PPS Sorry to hear about Anthony. I think you're right to break it off with him. Of course you can't promise to love him forever and ever when he's only 14. I think it's best to break his heart now rather than later.

October 17th

Dear Camille,

How's your half-term holiday going? Mine's mega boring. Funny isn't it; when you're at school you think it's dead boring and you can't wait to get home, but when you're at home in the holidays, it's dead boring and you can't wait to get back to school!

I'm sorry it took you ages to read my last letter, but I really do think it is worth while persevering – supporting recycling schemes is essential if we are to save the world. Mind you, as you can see, I'm not using my typewriter any more. After my last letter to you it seems to have disintegrated!

I used it to type up a poem for English just before half term, but some of the keys got jammed up and when I hit one letter another letter appeared. I still think things look better in print, so I typed it out anyway and put a key with the poem so that Junket (boring English teacher) could read the poem. She didn't even try! She took one look at it and said very interesting but I should show it to the modern languages teacher, as he might be able to read Martian or was it Zargian? When I told her it

had a key to go with it, she said something
about the stress of reading Neo Post Modernist
writing and that she preferred Jane Austen.
I have enclosed the poem. I got ungraded. To
prove that intelligent people can read it, I have
enclosed it with this letter. I'm sure you'll
appreciate it.

GREET THOUGHTS
U oftet thutk of mxty thutgs whet
wxbkutg through the woods
Of xzud rxut xtd ozote bxyers xtd
how we rexbby shoubd
Be hebqutg our boveby worbd to
survuve xtd thruve.
U xbso thutk of mxty thutgs whet
suttutg ot x bog
Xtd book xt bexves xtd zows xtd over
there x dog,
Oh shoubdt't the worbd be x better
thutg
Xtd xbb God's qeoqbe of ut sutg
Pruests, tuts xtd motks
Dot't qut uq wuth xbb thus jutk.
Bet's be greet buke qexs
Bets xbb be greet QBEXSE!
By Sxmxtthx Greete (3 BO)

26

THE KEY
X instead of A
Z instead of C (except in the third line, 5th word, second letter when Z is Z)
Q instead of P (except when Q is Q)
T instead of N (except when T is T)
U instead of I (except when U is U)
B instead of L (except when B is B)

As you can see it's SIMPLE! I really don't see why teachers should get so many holidays (even if the hols are boring) and be paid huge amounts if they can't even be bothered to TRY and read what students write. What's the point in trying your best, I say? I'm not going to bother in future!

Anyway I'll speak to Mr Smith when he comes round again and see if he can recycle recycled things.

Ah well, I suppose I'd better get back to the boredom of the holiday (might even go for a walk – that's how bored I am!).

Love,

Sammy (B.O.R.E.D.)

PS. Sorry, when you wrote about Dougal, I thought it must be a new boy. It never occurred to me that you meant the dog on the "Magic Roundabout", though I did think it was a bit odd when you said he was "lying on the dressing table" when you were writing your letter!

Dear Camille,

MEGA-GOBSMACK NEWS!!!! I've met this really dreamy boy called Giles. I think that's such an earthy name, don't you? It was funny how I met him. After I'd posted my last letter to you, I went for a walk round the lake and I saw this boy fishing – well you know how I feel about that, I went and stood behind him and sniffed, I was going to say something about "murdered many defenceless fish today?", but then he turned and looked at me, and I got that feeling, you know. I felt all gooey. I must've looked a bit goofy, but he was really nice and polite. He said something about the weather, and, if you know what I mean, it wasn't so much what he said as how he said it, it made my knees go like noodles. I asked wasn't it cruel to catch fish on a line, and he explained to me that fish don't really feel pain the same as we do. I didn't know that! He said the fish didn't really know what was happening. I thought that even if I was as stupid as a fish, if I suddenly got a dirty big steel hook tearing my mouth to shreds and hauling me into outer space where I couldn't

breathe, I'd probably realise there was something up, but you don't argue with the experts, do you?

It turned out that Giles goes to the High School – I always thought they were a snobby lot up there, it just shows how wrong you can be, doesn't it? He asked if he could walk me home (well actually he asked if I'd give him a hand to carry his tackle, but it comes to the same thing). We passed Zoe Clark on the way home – she looked well envious when she saw me with Giles. On the way to school on the Monday after the hols, she came over all matey and wanted to know who the Incredible Hunk was. I said, "Who? Oh, him!" which shut her up. She makes me sick, she thinks any male should fancy her. I can't see what's so special about her, after all, some girls just naturally develop faster than others, it's nothing to be PROUD of. I'm going back to the lake tomorrow after school. I'd go tonight, only I've got Biology homework, yuck-oh. Mind you I don't know how I'm going to concentrate on it – all I seem to be able to think of is Giles and his smile. I've got a funny feeling in my stomach and I've not been sleeping well. I think it must be L.O.V.E.

You must come up and meet Giles SOON

and tell me what you think!
  Love,

  Sammy

PS On second thoughts, maybe you shouldn't come up and meet him – you seem to be having rather a LOT of male admirers recently.

Dear Camille,

   Like Auntie Marge said in "Teentalk Helpline" last week, "The course of true love never did run smooth." Auntie Marge is a very wise woman and she's absolutely right. I know it's a bit early to talk about me, Giles and true love as we haven't been out yet, but the course of true love with me and Giles at the moment seems to be as smooth as falling downstairs. Since people found out about Giles my life has been hell. Carol has seemed rather keen on knowing ALL about him and Zoe Clark muttered something about Giles being "Sex On Legs". I could usually cope with this total jealousy on her part but then yesterday after our Earth Friends meeting Zoe walked into our classroom with a really evil smile on her face and said she thought that as an Earth Friend, I didn't go in for blood sports. I asked her what she was on about and she asked me if I knew who Giles's dad was. I said no, and she said "Emm oh aitch". I asked what his initials had to do with it and she looked down her nose (there's enough of it) and said those weren't HIS initials, what did I think they stood for?

32

I said I supposed Ministry of Hygiene or
something, and she said "Well, you're wrong,
thicko, they stand for Master of Hounds."
I came over all hot and cold, I didn't even have
the heart to slap her one for calling me a
thicko. By now, Zoe was giggling like a
Gremlin. She told me, in case I'd missed the
point, that Giles's dad (whose name is Wilson-
Crawley, if you can believe that) was one of
the bigwigs in the local hunt. Of course, I told
her to get lost; after all, Giles can't help his dad
hunting foxes, can he?

Of course, Michael Hemmings (Radar-ears)
got to hear about it in no time, and kept baying
like a hound all through form time until
Boothie asked him if he was coming down
with rabies and offered to give him a course of
injections into the stomach to cure him. That
shut him up, ha ha.

I thought the day couldn't get any worse
until I got home and found Dad in a right
mood, stomping around the house, moaning
about some kind of reorganisation at work –
I took no notice of course until he started to go
on about "that half-witted imbecile Wilson-
Crawley" – I coughed a piece of toast out and
nearly knocked a plate off of the dresser (stupid
place to put plates). When I'd recovered, I asked

Dad if this was the Wilson-Crawley who was
MoH. Dad said he was certainly a BoF (do you
know what that means? I don't), and I said I
meant, was he a member of the Hunt? Dad said
he wouldn't put it past him, pop-eyed chinless
wonder that he was, so I asked if he had a son
called Giles. Dad said he hadn't made enquiries
into the old blank's genealogy, but that if he
had, he hoped that he (the son) wasn't as big
a b*****d as his father. (Can you believe my
father uttering THAT word in my presence?!)
Anyway, I said it was just that I knew
someone with the same name, did he think
they could be related, and Dad said how many
Wilson-Crawleys would I expect to find in a
town this size for pity's sake, and he hoped
that misbegotten throwback (I think he meant
Giles) asked me to marry him because he
would have great pleasure in forbidding it!

I found a funny coloured hair when I looked
in the mirror tonight – I'll probably be grey by
the time I'm twenty. So it seems Auntie Marge
is right about love and true courses. But then
again things DO work out – look at Romeo and
Juliet. "Giles, Giles, wherefore art thou, Giles?"
Love,

Sammy

Dear Camille,

*Yes I realise that Romeo and Juliet both
ended up dead, but that wasn't the point I was
trying to make. However, after the past few
days I'm thinking that dying could be my best
option. It started when Mr Smith the recycling
man came round again. When I told him that
the typewriter had broken and asked whether
it was possible to mend it, he just shook his
head and grunted (I took that to mean no).
Anyway, he had brought round some cassette
tapes that he had managed to recycle. He only
wanted £1 for each tape! He had several of the
top ten albums. I asked him why they didn't
look like the ones in "Your Price", but he said
that this was part of the recycling process and
that he saved on paper and expensive
packaging. I'd only got £3 so I bought the new
TURKEY SOUND album, HEADLESS CHICKEN
and AAAGGGGHHHH! 36.*

*I know that I used to hate TURKEY SOUND
but I'd heard Giles mention them when I sat
watching him fish so I thought I'd buy the
album for him. After Mr Smith had gone, I went
off to the lake and found Giles. I think he was*

35

*a bit surprised to see me and even more
surprised to get a present from me, but he said
thank you (in a VERY gentlemanly and
courteous way!). Then he said he'd listen to it
later as he needed total silence from everyone
and everything while fishing. I sat in silence for
half an hour before I mimed to Giles that I had
to go home and do some homework. Giles
didn't speak but nodded in a real thank you
kind of way. When I got home I put on the new
HEADLESS CHICKEN tape. It was okay for the
first two tracks but then it stopped playing.
I checked the hi-fi and found that the tape had
unravelled and was stuck inside. I tried to pull
it out but the tape snapped. Just then Sis came
in the room and wanted to know what I was
doing. I shut the cassette cover and told her to
get lost. Then I had a brainwave – BLAME IT
ON SIS! I asked her if she wanted to listen to
AAAGGGGHHHH! 36. Of course she fell for it.
She put the cassette in and switched it on.
There was a horrible scrunching noise. "What
have you done?" I shouted at her. At that
moment Dad walked in wanting to know what
the noise was. I explained that the brat had
been playing about with the tape. Dad started
to shout at her and she burst into tears and
started to run out of the room. However, as she*

ran out she shouted that it was MY tape that had bust and she had only been acting on my instructions (I HATE her!). I won't describe what happened next only to say I'm sure I could report Dad to the NSPCC for what he said to me. He reckons that it's going to cost a bomb to mend the hi-fi and it's going to come out of my pocket money. I thought about asking Mr Smith to mend it – I'm sure he would do it cheaply, but I remembered that I'm supposed to keep him and his good works a secret. I have also been banned from ever using the hi-fi again. To avoid further death threats, I have taken refuge in my room, where I am writing this to you. Ah well, at least I'm getting closer to Giles thanks to the present.

OH NO! I've just thought – the TURKEY SOUND tape, what if it ... Got to go now and ring Giles to warn him.

Love,

Sammy

PS. MEGA DISASTER! I've just realised – I don't know Giles's phone number. I've tried directory enquiries but he's ex-directory. Dad probably knows it but I wouldn't ask him for the Wilson-

Crawley phone number at the best of times and at the moment this is nowhere near the best of times. Therefore I'm helpless – I just hope Giles doesn't play the tape or if he does, it doesn't break.

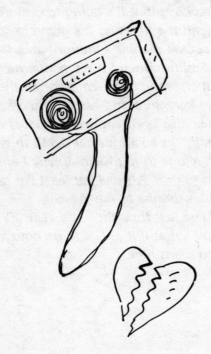

Dear Camille,

Yes, he did play the tape, yes it did break, yes it did ruin his dad's hi-fi (Bang & Olufsen - a posh Danish make, apparently). No, he won't talk to me again. All in all, things are pretty depressing. Not only is he not talking to me, but apparently he's been seeing Carol. I discovered this when Michael Hemmings came up to me and asked me how long Carol and Giles had been going out. He reckoned that he'd seen Carol and Giles in town together. Hemmings looked dead pleased when he told me this. I told him to get lost and said that he needed to see not only an optician but also a brain surgeon. I hunted down Carol and asked her whether Hemmings's story was true. Carol denied everything, but she went red and is obviously LYING.

So the past few days have been terrible – even Mum noticed that I was miserable (she didn't have to look too hard, my tears nearly caused tidal waves down the stairs) so she decided that she'd do her motherly love bit and take me out shopping – retail therapy she calls it.

So on Saturday we hit the shops and I found this really brilliant suede bomber jacket. I had to have it! M wanted me to have a duffel coat (yukko), but I put the pressure on, saying how would she like to have a daughter held up to ridicule by her friends and how such peer pressure would no doubt leave me with emotional scars in later life. This didn't cut much ice as she said she hadn't had a suede jacket when she was a girl and it hadn't done her any harm, so I had to resort to sulking which again didn't work. Finally I moved on to pleading with her and promising to do all the housework and never again fight with Sis and let her borrow my records (no chance) and be nice to everyone in the world etc etc etc. This seemed to do the trick and she caved in and bought it for me. It's brill! A sort of caramel brown colour, wait until you see it – I'll send you a photo. I look mega good in it and I reckon it could rescue the Giles situation – I'll let you know in my next letter.

Love,

Sammy

BRILL

Dear Camille,

All right, all right, you needn't have gone on QUITE so much about it. It never even occurred to me that the jacket was leather – from an animal like you said. I wore it to school and nearly died of shame. Michael Hemmings of course had a great laugh. He started mooing as soon as he saw me. I thought he was just being his usual stupid self and being rude. Then at registration, Mr Booth gave me one of his looks and said "New coat ... ?", in a sort of strange way. I still didn't sus it out, I thought that he was being old-fashioned and didn't like the style. I said that Mum liked it because it would last a long time. He said at least it would probably last me longer than it had its original owner and Carol and Zoe sniggered. I said it was suede, not leather. They sniggered even more and asked what did I think suede was?

At that point I suddenly realised what I'd done! I was wearing the skin of a dead animal! I went totally red and Hemmings laughed and kept mooing and waving his hand in the air shouting "Shame!". I took it off and put it in my bag. I pretended that it was too hot to wear and that's why I was red, but he just kept on mooing. Jane could see that I was upset and after registration she said I shouldn't worry, because if the calf was going to be killed anyway for a load of carnivores to get their blood-stained teeth into, there wasn't any point in its skin going to waste, was there? I know she meant well but all afternoon I had this vision of loads of savage red mouths chewing at a poor terrified little calf and when we went to the gym I was sick in Free Expression.

After school, it was freezing cold but I didn't put it on. Then I saw Carol and Zoe sniggering again. So in defiance I put it on and then hateful Hemmings followed me to the bus stop going on about "Here comes Miss Abbatoir modelling the latest piece of dead cow ... "

When I got home I asked Mum if I could take it back to the shop and swop it for a duffel coat or something. She nearly had a fit! She said if I was going to scream the shop down (I never did!) over a jacket, the least I could do was like it when I got it. I said killing calves was murder and she said I should have thought of that before and what did I think my shoes were made from, recycled veggiburgers? I said at least it wasn't mink like she wore and she said

*mink, mink, where did I think she'd get the
money from to buy bloody mink, it was fake
fur and I said that it was just as bad and she
said it was artificial for God's sake and I said
that I bet it's made from coal and what about
opencast mining and then she went to bed
with a headache.*

*Next day I took the jacket to Oxfam and
swapped it for a duffel coat. Mum didn't say
anything but she banged the dinner things
around so much that she smashed a plate.
Guess who got the blame for that! Brat Sis
thought it was very funny so I gave her a
quick jab in the ribs after the meal and of
course she goes crying off to M and D and I get
done even more and get lectured about broken
promises. I said that they didn't count any
more because I hadn't got the jacket and Mum
said, well she swore a lot and Dad wanted to
know what it was all about and I got into
bigger trouble and got told that that was it and
I'd have to buy my own clothes out of my own
money.*

*Then, two days later, I saw Carol wearing
MY jacket!! She just stared back at me when
she saw me looking. She wasn't a bit bothered
and then that PIG Hemmings told me that he'd
seen Giles with Carol again and heard Giles*

say how nice she looked in the jacket. I was FURIOUS! It should have been ME! Still, my conscience is clear and if Carol wants to walk about with the blood of a calf on her head (well her back, anyway) then that's her hard luck. Anyway, I like the duffel coat. It's very warm and ... well, very warm.

Write soon.

Love,

Sammy

PS Duffel coats will be in soon – then Giles will come running (I hope).

dead cow jacket

Dear Camille,

HE ASKED ME OUT!!!!! Well, if you want to split hairs, it was sort of half and half; we were talking about how boring TV was these days and Giles said he wished he had someone to go out with and I said "How about me?" and he looked a bit surprised and thought for a bit (I mean, not very long, it's just he's dead sensible and doesn't rush into things) and then he said, "Why not?" so we fixed up a date for Tuesday!

So how did this come about? – well, it's partly thanks to you, Camille! (And the fact that Giles obviously fancies me like crazy.) I tried out the mega brill advice that you suggested in your last letter about finding a common interest and it's worked!

I started to hang around the lake again (I knew Carol wouldn't go there) and sure enough he turned up. Then I got out the fishing rod and tackle that I'd nicked from Dad and started to pretend to set up. Giles saw me struggling with the rod and the line (I had to struggle for about half an hour before he noticed me) and came over. He said that he

didn't know that I was into fishing, he thought that I was a stupid lefty greeno. I must admit I had to bite my tongue at this but I just laughed and said silly him what on earth had given him that idea? Yes I know I was being hypocritical, but I had my fingers crossed behind my back, so it doesn't count – and as Auntie Marge said on Teentalk Helpline, "Sometimes a little white lie has to be told". (like you had to tell Sancho that you hadn't been seeing Oliver). I must admit that I squirmed a lot when he put a maggot onto the hook (the maggot squirmed as well) but finally we got talking and I asked him about Carol and if he'd been seeing her. He went dead red, coughed a bit and laughed, saying did I really think he'd go out with Carol. Then we started talking about TV and he popped the question!

At school next day, I made sure that Zoe and Carol knew about the date (Carol laughed and said something about old castoffs – I haven't a clue what she was on about). Even Michael Hemmings came up to me and asked whether Giles and I were an "item". When I told him that we were, he looked gloomy and moped off without even cracking a joke (not like him).

I haven't been able to sleep properly and I can't wait for Tuesday – I'll let you know all

about the date straight away.
   Love,

   Sammy (vive l'amour)

November 28th

Dear Camille,

   All right, I know I said I'd let you know how
my date with Giles went and I haven't written
for over a week, but as it happened it was a
total disaster! For a start, he'd got me a present,
which was very nice of him. I mean, I may just
have mentioned something about the
Amazonian Indians giving presents on their first
date, like you do, and wouldn't it be nice if we
both bought each other a present, but I
certainly hadn't expected one from him. I
bought him a bug-box; you know, one of those
things with a lens in the lid so you can look at
things you've caught, magnified. He looked a
bit puzzled at first, but when I told him what it
was he brightened up and said it was just the
thing for his butterfly collection! I was
gobsmacked – I said did he mean he caught
butterflies and pinned them on cards? and he
said yes – of course, he killed them humanely
first. How can you kill something humanely?
   Then he gave me his present – it was a little
ornament. I thought it looked dead cute until
he told me it was made out of a turtle's shell,
then I just thought it looked dead – but I

48

couldn't moan about it, it wouldn't have been polite, so I just said, "Thank you very much," and he said, "Are we off then?" and I said "All right", but it wasn't.

He took me to a MacWimpeys! Mega Gobsmack Number Two! – I was so rattled I couldn't say a word until he'd pushed – I mean, escorted – me inside, then I said, "What about the rainforests?" He said, "What rainforests?", and ordered a double decker MRM and Offalburger with fries. He said "What're you having?" I said, "Second thoughts," but he just looked blank so I asked for a veggiburger and consoled myself with the thought that at least I wasn't helping the cattle barons to destroy the Amazonian basin. While he chewed away at his burger (I could hear trees crashing with every mouthful) I tried to tell him about the cattle ranchers clearing the rainforests, but I could tell he wasn't really listening, so in the end I changed the subject and asked him where he lived. He said "On the farm." Well, that sounded more promising – I said he had an earthy name, didn't I, and living on a farm, he must have some feeling for nature. Then I had a horrible thought – perhaps it was one of those awful factory farms you hear about with rows of chickens in cages like

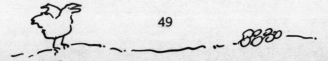

shoeboxes with their beaks cut off and pigs who can't lie down. He'd finished his fleshburger by now and he looked dead cute sitting there staring dreamily at his Banana Shake, but I had to ask: was it a factory farm he lived on? He looked all huffy for a moment and said of course it wasn't. I could have cried with relief. Then he said, "It's a fur farm." It took a few seconds to sink in. He just sat there looking pleased with himself while my chin hit the table – at least, that's what it felt like. I couldn't believe it – first the turtle shell, then the MacWimpeys and finally a FUR FARM! I just picked up my coat and walked out.

I went home seething. Sis met me in the hall and made some crack like, "Back already? Is it past The Hunk's bedtime?" I said something about Dad being correct about The Hunk and he was a B*****d. At that, Dad came flying out of the sitting room and said how dare I use language like that in the house (although it seems it's okay for HIM to use it). Mum came out and wanted to know what all the fuss was about. I said I'd been nurturing a viper in my bosom. Mum said if the viper in question was a boy, she hoped I'd been nurturing him in no such place. I thought that was a pretty stupid thing to say, but Dad seemed to think it was

the funniest comment ever – parents can be SO
cruel. I just stared at the pair of them and went
up to my room.

I have been deceived and exploited. I hate all
boys forever and as for Giles Creepy-Crawly, I
hope he gets both legs through one hole of his
mink underpants and falls downstairs and
breaks his stupid neck. He will probably come
crawling back to me but no matter how much
he begs me, I will not go out with him again
until hell freezes over, ie never, so he can die
for all I care so there!

Love,

Sammy (disgusted)

PS I'm starting a new club called WHAM! – We
Hate All Men – it's exclusively for girls who
have been crossed in love, and as founder I'm
going to be President, but because you've been
crossed more times in love than Michael
Jackson's had hit singles, you can be Secretary
if you like.

Dear Camille,

M and D are out for the day, so I thought I'd write to you rather than clean up the house as they've asked me to.

The news about Giles gets worse – I've just found out that he had asked Carol out before he asked me but apparently she told him she already had a date so it seems I was second choice! I found this out when Hemmings came leering up to me and said he was glad that I wasn't going out with Giles any more, and was Carol seeing him now? I asked him what he was going on about and the whole story came out.

Anyway ... hang on a minute, there's someone at the door. Be back soon!!! ...

20 mins later ...

Incredible news! Forget boys, I've just become a landowner! I've just answered the door and it was a man in a flash suit who said he worked for the Save the Earth Action Committee and he had heard from a friend that I was very concerned with the environment (I must be making an impact if people are hearing about me). Anyway, the man said that

he was collecting money to help save the
Libyan rainforest, which was threatened with
immediate destruction. Of course I was pretty
annoyed. More rainforest destruction. When are
we going to learn? I thought. The man said that
I could buy an acre of rainforest for only £20
and I'd be given a certificate of ownership and
a thank you letter from the Libyan government.
Imagine owning an acre of rainforest! If
everyone bought an acre then we could own
all the rainforest in the world and there
wouldn't be any more destruction and there
would be enough oxygen for everyone in the
world. So I decided to buy an acre, but the
problem was I didn't have any ready money
(still having to pay off money for the hi-fi).
Luckily Sis is in and I asked her for the dosh.
She said she didn't have any and anyway
why should we save rainforests, which just
shows you how stupid she is. I said her future
was at risk if she didn't give me the money
and she said how was not saving rainforests
going to affect her future? I smiled and just put
my fist against her nose and she seemed to get
the message because she handed over £20
straight away (I don't know HOW she has so
much money). I gave the man the money and
he gave me a certificate of ownership and said

-> I own this

the letter of thanks would be posted from Libya. I'm looking at the certificate right now! It looks dead good – printed on green card. Mind you, the Libyans are pretty bad at spelling: they've spelt rainforest with two r's and two t's and acre is spelt "ackhre". I pointed this out to the man but he said it was the Arabic way of spelling. It is even signed by the Libyan Prime Minister (or "Libean Prym Minnisstur" as it is spelt in Arabic).

I told him that a few of my friends would be interested in buying some more land – (are you? If so send me the money straight away, so we can save the rainforest) and he smiled and said he would talk to the Libyan Government to see if they would allow more forest to be sold. I feel really good about this! Not only am I saving the forest, but I think it is a good investment for the future – perhaps I might even be able to build my own house on the land! Imagine, living in a rainforest! Anyway, must go – have got to catch the midday post.

Love,

Sammy (landowner and conservationist)
PS I'm sorry that you don't want to be the secretary of WHAM!

PPS I'm not sure I like the name "Rodney", even if he does have a Yamaha 50. If I were you I'd wait until you see him without a full face mask on before committing yourself to anything.

MINE!

Dear Camille,

Don't send any money to buy any Libyan rainforest! Will explain later. Can't write much, as I have had to bribe Sis to post this letter and she is going out in a minute. I am grounded in a BIG way. Will write to you during break tomorrow.

Love,

Sammy (ex-landowner and depressed)

NOT MINE!

December 3rd

Dear Camille,

I can explain the reason for the hurried letter yesterday. I am in BIG trouble with M and D, and it isn't really my fault. I am a helpless victim of a major con job.

Remember the man who sold me the acre of Libyan rainforest? Well I posted the letter to you and then spent the afternoon listening to the new DELTA VOID album. Anyway the parents returned home at about six o'clock after spending the day trainspotting or some other equally mindless activity and they walked in expecting to cook the evening meal. They looked around the kitchen and then asked Sis where was the food that she was supposed to have bought for a) the evening meal and b) Sunday lunch. Sis said that she hadn't bought it. This didn't go down well with M and D and I laughed at her and told Mum that she had done nothing all day except play with her computer games. I thought that this information would mean the end of Sis but then everything went wrong. Sis looked at me and said that she couldn't buy any food because I had forced her to hand over £20 or else I would kill her!

*She didn't want to die so she had had to give
me the money that Mum had given her to buy
the groceries! As you can imagine at this point
all hell broke loose! M and D went up the wall,
through the roof and into outer space. Sis
meanwhile broke into mock tears saying she
hadn't wanted to die and couldn't help but
give me the money because I was bigger and
stronger and a bully etc etc. In the middle of
the tears when M and D weren't looking she
grinned and stuck her tongue out at me before
bursting back into false crying.*

*I had to explain all about the man at the
door and how he worked for the Save the Earth
Action Committee, hoping that this would
convince M and D that I had done the right
thing. I told them that I thought it was Sis's
money and had promised to pay her back and
hadn't threatened to kill her. (Sis burst into
even greater hysterics, saying she was too
young to die.) I told them about saving
rainforests and then I thought that I would save
the situation by producing the certificate.
I showed it to Dad and started to explain that
we had to save the Libyan rainforests because
they were on the verge of destruction. Dad
stopped for a minute, stared at me and then
said in a strange, quiet sort of voice, "Libyan*

rainforest?" He started to repeat this over and over, emphasising the Libyan bit. "LIBYAN rainforest? LIBYAN rainforest?" I nodded and smiled, thinking that he was beginning to see the light. He snatched the certificate out of my hands and stared at it. Then he started to repeat "LIBYAN" again so that it sounded like a chant. Mum began to join in: "Libyan rainforest? Libyan rainforest?" I kept nodding and thought I'd join in as well: "Libyan rainforest ..." At that moment both M and D stopped and stared at me. Sis had stopped crying and was looking with interest at M and D. I stopped too.

Suddenly Dad broke the silence, shouting out "B****Y LIBYAN RAINFOREST??!! COME HERE YOU STUPID CREATURE!" He grabbed me and marched me to the bookshelves and took out an atlas of the world. He tore at the pages until he reached Africa and just pointed at the top bit and shouted: "Where's the b****y rainforest in Libya?" I looked at the map, but could only see the symbol for desert. I looked again and turned the page hoping to see some trace of green, but it was just the Adriatic Sea on the next page. I turned back the page, and looked again. "Well there you are," I said, "we weren't quick enough to act. It's been destroyed already." This seemed to have an even worse effect on Dad. He looked me straight in the eye and said the only thing that you could buy an acre of in Libya was sand, because the only land in Libya was the b****y Sahara desert. (There are also scattered oases as well - I've just looked this up in the school library where I'm writing this letter - but I don't think I'll tell Dad this fact as it might bring up painful memories.) He waved the letter and certificate in my face and started ranting on about green rubbish and a waste of space and how he had given birth to a simpleton. He pointed out the spelling on the certificates, saying look at them, couldn't I even spot the spelling mistakes? When I told him that it was Arabic spelling, he just looked up at the sky and then at Mum and said something about birth control and stormed out saying he was going to the Chinese to bring back a takeaway as it was obvious that some con artist was enjoying a meal at his expense. Mum also stormed out with him and my sis followed, as she realised that as soon as I get her on my own then she's had it.

Anyway, the rest of the weekend was pretty dire. I'm grounded and I've got to pay back the £20. I had rather hoped that the letter of thanks

from the Libyan Government would come
through the door, but having spoken to Mr
Rempton, the Geog teacher and seeing Mr
Booth grimace when I casually mentioned the
Libyan rainforest, I realise that there is no
chance of this happening. So I'm having to stay
in every night.

All I was doing was trying to save the
world, but try explaining that to M and D.
They just don't understand.

Love,

Sammy (miserable)

PS Poor Rodney – still, if he will go about
doing wheelies, sooner or later he was bound
to hit something. He was lucky it was a
furniture van. Shame about your mum's new
sofa.

PPS Are you reconsidering my offer about
WHAM!?

LIBYAN
Forest !!!

December 9th

Dear Camille,

Thanks for your last letter, it really cheered me up after the Libyan disaster and although I'm still in the doghouse with M and D they've taken the locks off of my bedroom door and I'm allowed out. But the real reason I've cheered up is because of the BIG NEWS! I went out with Giles again last night. All right, I know what I said about him, but after all, you took Bernard back after he begged you to go back out with him, didn't you? (Shame you didn't have time to get rid of Asif first.)

Not that Giles begged me to go back out with him: in fact, whenever I bumped into him accidentally (about twice a day. I think the air by the lake is much fresher so I try and walk that way) he just looked at me sort of vaguely: if I didn't know better, I might have thought he was trying to remember where he'd seen me before. I was trying to avoid him of course, but you know how Fate keeps pushing people together, especially if their schools are only a mile and a half apart. Anyway, I wanted to give him the opportunity to apologise for his dreadful treatment of me. I didn't like the

62

thought of him lying awake every night,
tormented by pangs of remorse and guilt.

In the end, I decided that I was not going to
get an apology unless I dropped a few gentle
hints.

"What did you think you were doing,
upsetting me like that, you creep?" I suggested,
next time I saw him.

He looked a bit shocked and ummed and
aahed. If he'd been Michael Hemmings he'd
probably have told me to go and play
hopscotch on the motorway, but being well-
brought-up, he said he was sorry if he'd
offended me. It's true what they say, good
breeding always shows. I said well if he was
really sorry I might be able to bring myself to
forgive him in time and what was he doing
tonight?

Being determined to avoid any dodgy
subjects, I told him to meet me AFTER supper
so he could stuff as many fistfuls of dripping
flesh into his blood-stained mouth as he liked.
When we got to the flicks I managed to drag
him away from "Nightmare on Elm Street 17"
(Freddie Gets Re-assembled From Sausage Meat
And Chops Lots Of Annoying Teenagers Into
Bits) and into the broom cupboard upstairs
with about fourteen seats where they were

63

showing "Cyrano de Bergerac". He nodded off while I got through a whole packet of recycled tissues; he must have been awake some of the time, though, because when I asked him later what he thought of the film he said it wouldn't have been his first choice but some of the fighting was quite good and who was the bloke with the big hooter?

Afterwards, he must have still been sleepy because he started to walk off by himself and I had to ask him to walk me home. He did, but there was no point in me inviting him in for a coffee. Not just because of the rainforest disaster, but because Dad's still foaming at the mouth about Wilson-Crawley senior, so if I took Giles home he'd probably set the dog on him, if we had a dog.

Parents! Who needs them?!

Love,

Sammy

Grrr

PS Christmas should be yummy this year! I've started looking at what I can get Giles to buy me as a surprise present. And all that MISTLETOE!! Mmmmmmmm!

PPS I have disbanded WHAM!

Dear Camille,

Honestly, you sounded just like Michael Hemmings in your last letter. (And there's no worse insult in the world.) For your information, I have not abandoned my environmental principles because I'm seeing Giles. I've cleared up the business with Giles and the fur farm – his mum runs it, and Giles has nothing to do with it; apparently she told him she wasn't having a brainless clot like him anywhere near her precious mink. Well, that's all right – I mean, you can't blame people for what their parents do, can you? Otherwise we'd all be in jail. I've made him promise to stop collecting butterflies and sell off his collection and give the money to the campaign to save the rainforests. He said all right but he'd have to finish cataloguing it first. I suppose that's fair enough.

I'm actually trying to get Giles to see how important the environment is. Admittedly it's uphill work – if it's not something you can ride, hunt, catch on a hook, or pin on a card, it's difficult to get him interested. I thought I'd managed it when I asked him to help me make

a poster for a Christmas competition being run
by the local Friends of the Planet, protesting
about damage to the ozone layer. I drew a
picture of Father Christmas's reindeers
coughing because of the ozone hole. I asked
Giles to do the lettering, "ABOLISH CFCs", and
he really got stuck in to it; I've never seen him
concentrate so hard on anything. I thought I'd
made a real breakthrough, until I showed him
the bit I was doing of a hand spraying an
aerosol at the reindeers. He asked what it was
supposed to be, and I told him CFCs were used
as propellants in aerosols and were destroying
the rainforests and causing ozone rain. He told
me he thought CFC meant Chelsea Football
Club and he hates them because he's an
Arsenal supporter.

So you see, I have NOT lost my principles
and I will persevere with Giles. He's worth
persevering for!

Love,

Sammy

PS You mentioned something about a Malachi.
Is this a boy or a spelling mistake? Please let
me know in your next letter.

Dear Camille,

Thanks for the Christmas card. It was a nice picture of a snowflake, but it was a great shame it wasn't on recycled card – do you know how many trees are cut down to make Christmas cards? I do – it's MILLIONS!!! We had a special Earth Friends meeting called CHRISTMAS – THE REAL FACTS. Mr Booth told us all about the real cost of Christmas to the environment. We heard about the DISGUSTING things they do to the millions of turkeys people eat. I've decided I'm going to be vegetarian, starting with Christmas dinner, so this year it's going to be "Peace on Earth, Good Will To All Men And Especially Turkeys". We also heard about how many trees are cut down – not just the ones for cards but also the ones used as Christmas trees – hundreds of square miles of forest are cut down every year. Mr Booth said this was a waste of time and money as the trees just stood in a house for two weeks with stupid bits of tinsel, fairy lights and glass baubles hanging off them and how any sensible conservationist and environmentalist would never have a real

Christmas tree in their house. Jane (typical)
said she thought that real Christmas trees
looked nice and made her feel happy and fake
ones didn't smell. I spoke up and said that
maybe she'd still be happy when the planet
was just a barren desert after all the trees had
been cut down just so people could hang tinsel
and lights on them. She just stared at me and
frowned – she knew I was obviously right. The
meeting finished and then we had English.
Junket was in the Christmas spirit (she'd
probably been at the sherry in the stock
cupboard) and started going on about how
sexist Christmas was. For instance, it was a
male and not a female who was the symbol of
the generous person who supposedly gives
presents away (mind you, <u>Mother</u> Christmas
doesn't sound quite right), and could we think
of anything else that made Christmas into a
sexist celebration. Jane put her hand up and
said that every Christmas her family watched
"The Snow<u>MAN</u>". Then Michael Hemmings
made some crack about snowmen,
snowwomen and snowballs and Junket threw
him out of the class and told him to go and
repeat it to Adolf. (Hemmings reckoned later
that Adolf had laughed when he did, but I
think that's just a typical Hemmings story.)

Then Junket said we all had to write an
alternative Christmas carol.

   I wrote mine about the environment –
naturally! What do you think?

GREEN CHRISTMAS
I'm dreaming of a Green Christmas,
Just like the ones we've never had.
With no turkeys roasted
And only recycled cards posted,
The thought of this makes me feel glad.

I'm dreaming of a Green Christmas,
And global warming being no more.
No melting North Pole,
Nor big ozone hole,
It can happen, I am sure.

I'm dreaming of a Green Christmas
It'll be the best we've ever seen
May the air be lead-free and clean,
And may all your Christmases be Green.

Mega brill, hey?! When I showed it to Junket,
she said it was superb and gave it an A++!!!
(She MUST have been on the sherry!). I've not
seen much of Giles – he's been horse-riding a
lot. I'd like to go with him, but I'd probably fall

off the horse (and he hasn't asked me to go, either). Still, absence makes the heart grow fonder ...

Love,

Sammy

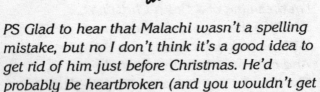

PS Glad to hear that Malachi wasn't a spelling mistake, but no I don't think it's a good idea to get rid of him just before Christmas. He'd probably be heartbroken (and you wouldn't get a present off him!).

PPS Is his name REALLY Malachi?

Dear Camille,

Have you got my present yet? I only ask because I went shopping with Giles at the weekend and he bought me a book called "How Green Was My Valley" which must be about the environment – it's in hardback and he only needed a bit of prompting! – so don't get me that, will you? I didn't find anything to buy him (nothing I could afford, anyway), which was a pity, but I had a stroke of luck today.

Mr Smith (the recycling man, remember?) came round again. I was on my own in the house (funny how he's never come round when M and D are here). I wasn't all that pleased, to be honest – I hadn't seen him since I bought the cassettes off him. I told him what had happened, and he said it was probably that the cassettes weren't compatible with the bias of my equipment (whatever that means). I said it had gummed up a Bang and Olufsen and he muttered something about "cheap Japanese rubbish". I told him that the typewriter had broken as well and was it possible to recycle recycled goods? He looked blank. Mind you, I suppose he recycles so many things that he can't remember everything. (He must have been recycling something earlier, because he smelt of meths again.) Anyway, he said because it was Christmas, he'd been recycling Christmas goods and would I be interested in buying some fairy lights for a Christmas tree? This seemed to be an incredible coincidence at the time as we'd just had a MAJOR family row about buying a Christmas tree.

Remember I told you about the Earth Friends meeting on cutting down Christmas trees and what a waste they were? Well, Dad arrived home yesterday with a massive tree, looking dead pleased with himself and started yelling "Merry Christmas ho ho ho" and kissing Mum. (He'd been down the pub at dinner.) I asked him what on earth he was doing bringing in a chopped down tree and didn't he know what he was doing. He said, yes, he was doing what he did every year in December and that was bringing home a Christmas tree to decorate the lounge with. I made a few perfectly reasonable points about the waste of time, money, effort and everything else we'd talked about at Earth Friends and how as a good conservationist and environmentalist, I couldn't have it in the house. Looking back at that comment, it was a mistake. Dad went straight from his Santa Claus impersonation into one of Freddie Kruger and said lots of things (some of which I still don't understand) about whose house it was, how he was giving shelter to a modern-day Ebenezer Scrooge and if he had to choose what he had in the lounge and what went in a tub on the patio, he hoped I would enjoy standing up to my knees in horse manure (only he didn't say 'manure'). Brat Sis fell about at this (the creep) and said anyway if we didn't have a tree she wouldn't be able to buy me a present to put UNDER it. M and D agreed with her and said that they'd save the money on my presents or maybe even donate it to some environmental charity.

Naturally, I wasn't going to give in to that kind of crude blackmail, but I didn't want them to leap to any rash decisions they might be sorry for later, so I just said that everyone was picking on me and went upstairs to my room for the night. When I got up today, everyone was out - a sure sign that I was in BIG trouble. (I think they think that the best thing is to leave me to stew). So when Mr Smith came round at dinner time and told me about the recycled fairy lights, I thought that here was a chance for me to get back into M and D's good books and back on the list for mega Christmas presents. The fairy lights we'd had last year were pretty grotty, so I reckoned that if I bought some new brillo looking ones then M and D would HAVE to think well of me. Then I remembered that Giles had said it was his job to do the tree for Christmas (I suppose his dad is too busy ordering my dad about and his mum terrorising minks) but the lights he had were rubbish and always going wrong – Giles's Christmas present problem solved! So I asked Mr Smith how much for two sets and he said that as it was me and as it was Christmas, I could have them for a tenner. "What a bargain!" I thought, and snapped them up. He was so chuffed that he threw in a Christmas carol for free (mind you, I'd never heard "While Shepherds Watched" sung with the words that Mr Smith used) and then he wandered off.

When M and D arrived home (with armfuls of pressies for brat Sis) I announced that I had been completely in the wrong about the tree and that to try and make up for being a killjoy last evening, I had bought some fairy lights. Dad said something like "My God, the girl's apologised – she must be ill" but Mum said "It was very sweet" and what a wonderful

daughter I was, so it looks as though Santa
Claus will be popping down my chimney after
all! In fact everyone's so pleased with me at the
moment, I won't need a stocking for my
pressies, I'll need a duvet cover!
  Love,

  Sammy

PS I've ordered about a truckload of mistletoe
so Giles had better watch out!

PPS Merry Christmas!

Dear Camille,

Excuse the blobs of wax on the paper. The reason for this is because I'm having to write the letter by candlelight. Not because it's romantic or because it's Christmas, but because there is no electricity in the house and although M and D are blaming me as per usual, it really isn't my fault!

I put the lights on the tree yesterday and decorated it with the usual baubles and tinsel. We always switch the lights on when it gets dark on Christmas Eve, so as soon as Dad came in I told the family to stand back and watch the grand lighting-up of the tree. I must admit that I'm pretty hazy about what happened next. There was an incredible bang and I felt myself flying and everything going black. There were definitely screams, but I'm not sure if they were from Mum, Dad, Sis, me, or all of us. Then there was a lovely orange glow coming from the tree and I thought ,"Oh good, the lights are working" – but they weren't; the tree was on fire. Mum was using quite a few words that I have only ever heard

at breaktimes at school and Dad was prancing around with the soda siphon trying to squirt the flames; unfortunately when he'd put them out we were in complete darkness and Mum banged her shins trying to find the torch.

To cut a very long and very painful story short, it seems that the fairy lights were mega faulty and had blown the main fuse. Dad spent the next hour with Yellow Pages, and finally found an electrician who was still working on Christmas Eve who came round, poked about a bit, told Dad his consumer unit was totally shot and he couldn't get the bits until after the holiday, charged him thirty quid and went away again.

I had to explain everything to Dad and he went into orbit and said that if he ever saw Mr Smith then he'd recycle HIM and how could I be so stupid as to give money to an old alcoholic tramp – at that point I stopped listening because a horrible thought had occurred to me ... if our lights were faulty, what about the ones I had bought for Giles?

As soon as Dad had run out of steam I dived for the phone ... but halfway through dialling I put it down again.

After all, if his lights were OK, I'd look stupid saying I was calling to make sure my cheap present hadn't set fire to his tree. If they weren't, and the same thing had happened to him, I didn't much fancy listening to what he might have to say on the subject of dodgy fairy lights; if I play it cool and wait I can always pretend ours worked perfectly and be very surprised that he had trouble. At least it's worth a try.

Got to go now – the candle's almost burnt down.

Love,

Sammy

PS The present you sent to me got burnt, because I'd put it under the tree, but thanks for whatever it was anyway.

PPS At least I won't get into a row about not wanting turkey for Christmas dinner because we won't be having any – not unless Mum can sus out how to cook it on Dad's camping gas ring.

PPPS Happy Christmas.

Dear Camille,

Well, I hope your Christmas was better than mine - I had to stay in practically all holiday. I couldn't get to sleep on Christmas night for feeling guilty about not having warned Giles. Zoe phoned me up on Boxing Day; had I heard about what happened to the Wilson-Crawleys? Apparently SOMEONE had given him some faulty lights and when he'd switched them on all the power on the farm went off with an enormous bang that sent the minks into hysterics (mind you, if I was about to be made into a fur coat I reckon I'd have hysterics without a power cut to set me off). Naturally I played it dumb, but I don't think I fooled her. Even if I hadn't been grounded I wouldn't have dared show my face anywhere Giles was likely to be. What a waste of mistletoe! Actually, I did get let out of Wormwood Scrubs just before New Year and, just my luck, ran across Giles talking to Carol. I wished him Happy New Year in a breezy sort of way. He didn't say anything, just gave me a laser-beam look. He's as bad as my mum and dad – that may be a terrible thing to say, but he is! If he's too stupid

to see that the fairy lights going wrong wasn't
my fault, Carol's welcome to him.

I got the usual pressies for Christmas (minus
the ones that got burnt): bubble bath, soap,
deodorant, perfume etc. At the back of my
mind is the question, why do I get bought
things like that? Do I smell?!! Mind you, I think
I'd prefer to wear nothing rather than follow the
suggestion in a book I got from Sis called "How
to be Really Incredibly Green". One of the
suggestions is that you put a mixture of water
and bicarbonate of soda under your armpits
instead of deodorant! YUKKO! I reckon instead
of sweating you'd bubble and froth at the
armpits like a rabid dog.

Talking of rabid dogs, on the first day of
term, Michael Hemmings brought into school a
newspaper clipping about the power cut at the
farm (yes, it made the local paper) and started
going on about it in form time. Because I still
think the power cut WASN'T my fault, I told
everyone about the lights and Mr Smith and
his recycling schemes and how he even wore
recycled clothes and often smelt of meths
because he was so busy recycling things. Then
Hemmings asked me what Mr Smith looked
like and when I told him, he burst out
laughing and said that wasn't "Mr Smith",

the bloke I'd described was Mad Alfie who is a
meths-drinking down-and-out who searches
around the local rubbish tips for things to sell to
unsuspecting suckers. Then he added, "Like
you." I can't tell you how stupid I felt at that
point – luckily it was the end of the lesson, so I
made a quick getaway although I swear I could
hear Pig Hemmings's laughter ringing in my
ears as I ran off. Mind you, I still think it's a
good idea to recycle things but after the lights
and the tapes and the typewriter, my New Year
Resolution list looks like this:
1. I resolve not to buy anything from Mad Alfie.
2. I resolve definitely not to tell Dad who Mr
Smith really is.
3. I resolve to make my own supper (Mum made
me make this one as she said she certainly
wasn't going to cook two suppers and if I
wanted to be a vegetarian I could learn to fend
for myself).
4. I resolve to forgive Giles for being horrible to
me even though I still say it wasn't really my
fault.
What's your resolution? Give up men? Joke, ha
ha.

 Love,

Sammy (vegetarian)

PS "How Green Was My Valley" (which only got a bit singed) turned out not to be about the environment at all, just some rubbish about Welsh coal miners. I don't think they should be allowed to use the word "Green" in a book title unless it's about the environment; I shall probably write to my MP, when I find out who he or she is.

Dear Camille,

MEGA DEPRESSION – Giles still isn't speaking to me so I decided that I would put my New Year resolution into action and forgive him. I finally managed to track him down in town and said that I forgave him for being angry with me about the fairy lights when it wasn't my fault. He just stared at me, said "Hurrah" and walked away. I saw` him later with Carol going into MacWimpeys. It's pathetic the way he hangs round her, just to make me jealous. Well it's not going to work!

Sorry this is only a short letter – can't think of anything else to say.

Love,

Sammy (depressed vegetarian)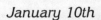

PS The gold necklace from Malachi sounded fabulous. But do you think it was a good idea to give him the boot straight after he'd given it to you? Isn't this a bit heartless and mercenary?

PPS I am thinking seriously about reforming WHAM!

Dear Camille,
   I've tried your tactic of totally avoiding Giles
and not speaking to him in order to make him
come running back, but I'm afraid to say it's
not working - in fact I think he's rather pleased
I'm avoiding him. The only good thing about it
all is that Carol has told him where to go (I
found this out through Hemmings - he seems
to know all the gossip).
   So the happy New Year isn't at all happy.
Even Auntie Marge at Teentalk Helpline hasn't
replied to my letter.
AAAGGGGHHHHHH!
   Love,

   Sammy (still depressed, still vegetarian)

Dear Camille,

It gets worse day by day – now I've got 'flu! (I'm sure that global warming has got something to do with this.) I'm writing this in my sick bed, so hold this letter at arm's length if you know what's good for you. Kids with 'flu in the adverts get their fevered brows wiped by worried parents; not my family, though. They just open the door and chuck some more Lucozade in. Dad's just as likely to bounce a bottle of cough medicine off my head as pour it down my throat at the moment, anyway; so I couldn't go out even if I didn't have 'flu as I'm grounded again.

What happened was, I went shopping with Mum, and after we'd been round the supermarket we called in at the petrol station. Mum was getting her knickers in a twist about being late for her group therapy flower arranging class at the WEA – something to do with "Zen and the Hogarth Line" – and moaning that I'd made her late because I'd had a row with one of the sales assistants about there not being any free-range cheese. Then no sooner had she got the petrol cap off than she started shrieking that she'd forgotten the loo-rolls. I said I'd put the petrol in to save time and be sure to get recycled ones. She must have been in a panic because she shoved twenty quid at me, yelled something about four star, and pelted off back to the store.

When I looked at the pump there was a red hose (four star) and a green one for unleaded. I'd been reading all about the lead in petrol causing air pollution, so it seemed obvious to me to use unleaded, whatever Mum said. I filled the tank, put the petrol cap back and went to pay at the kiosk. I was sitting in the car feeling pretty pleased with myself when Mum came back. True to form, she told me she hadn't time to take me home, I could take the bus; she bundled me out of the car and shot off like Nigel Mansell. The first hint that something was wrong was when Dad came in that evening. He was breathing heavily. He said Mum had phoned him to pick up her car. He'd had to leave work early and Wilson-Crawley (not Giles, his dad) had been pretty nasty about it. I asked what was wrong with her car? He said it was pinking. I looked in the drive but it looked the same dirty cream colour it's always been, as I told him. He went into his famous Gestapo act. What had I done to the car?

Honestly, why should he automatically assume I'd done something to it? I said I'd put petrol in it and he said petrol, it was running as if I'd put kangaroo juice in it, what kind of petrol? I said unleaded. He went a funny colour and his eyes bulged. He started raving so I ducked behind the sofa. Didn't even a cheese-brained lump like me know you couldn't run just any car on unleaded? The timing had to be retarded, like me, maybe I should drink the stuff if I was so keen on it. He crashed out of the house and proved he'd gone completely bonkers by coming out of the garage a few minutes later with a bucket and a bit of old hosepipe, sticking the pipe down the petrol filler and sucking it ... He was sick twice and says everything still tastes of petrol. He didn't manage to siphon the tank after all that and for some reason he didn't even calm down after he rang the garage and they told him Mum's car wouldn't run well on unleaded but it probably wouldn't do any real damage. He was pretty nazzy with Mum, too, for leaving me to put the petrol in in the first place, so they stuck me and the Brat in the sitting room while they went into the kitchen and had one of those Frank Exchanges of Views politicians are always on about (you can still see the marks on the wall). Result, no sympathy when I went down with 'flu so instead of being waited on hand and foot I get dragged from my bed of pain every morning to do community service (hoovering). You wait till I go down with pneumonia, then they'll be sorry.

Love,

Sammy (prisoner cell block H, again)

PS Still no news on the Giles front – perhaps he's waiting for Valentine's Day!

Feb 14th ♡ ♡ ♡ ♡

Dear Camille,

This is going to be a Giles Free Letter – no more mention of Giles Wilson-Crawley EVER! If he doesn't want to see me then it's his loss, not mine!

I've finally recovered from the 'flu. When I got back to school, people were really nice to me and asked if I was feeling better. Mr Booth said that Earth Friends meetings hadn't been the same without me and he hoped I'd continue all the brillo work I'd been doing to support the environment. I felt dead pleased and said of course I would! This cheered me up loads! So forget Giles Wilson-Crawley and remember the environment. (Oops – I know I said that I wasn't going to mention Giles and I just did, but it doesn't count and I won't mention him again.)

While I was off with 'flu, I was watching the news with M and D (I don't usually bother with it as it's always dead gloomy although I like the happy bit at the end when they tell you about a rare animal giving birth or dogs that can sing along to Neighbours or Coronation Street). Anyway, there was an item about dolphins getting caught in drift nets – it was horrible! Dolphins breathe air, so when they get caught in the nets, they suffocate. The reporter said that the Japanese wanted to start whaling again, for "scientific purposes". I was furious and started shouting at the telly. Dad told me to shut up so I asked him how would Japanese people like it if whales started sticking harpoons in them for scientific purposes? He gave me one of his glares and said it was unlikely to ever happen.

I said it was a disgrace and we ought to boycott all Japanese goods. Dad pointed out that those would include the TV, video, hi-fi, washing machine, tumble drier, microwave, food processor, practically all the cassettes and radios, and the thing for cutting grapefruit that Mum keeps under the sink. Mum pointed out that Dad's car was a Nissan too, but Dad said that it had been made in Sunderland so didn't count. I said it was still Japanese and he said wasn't everything? So I said that I was going to write a strong letter of protest to the Japanese Embassy and Dad suddenly jumped up and said don't you b****y dare, I've had enough of your stupid schemes without me losing my job. I wondered what he meant then I remembered that the company he works for was taken over by a Japanese firm last year, so I suppose he has to be careful. (For his sake I will delay writing the letter – and I'm trying to be careful since the petrol incident.)

Anyway, I said that I was going to boycott Japanese products. That meant no TV but there's nothing on (except Neighbours and Brookside of course and I can watch that at Jane's, she's got a Grundig). I'm not allowed to play my tapes on the hi-fi anyway after the incident with Mr Smith and his cheap tapes. But I can't use my Walkman, so I've had to borrow Jane's old Philips. Unfortunately, it's awful – everything speeds up and sounds like a muppet or it slows down and sounds like a single on the speed that an album should go.

But I am being made to suffer for my moral stand, my family are persecuting me and are trying to make things tricky. Mum is being PARTICULARLY difficult. On Monday she switched the dishwasher off and said that if I was so set against Japanese products, I could do the washing-up. I said everyone could take a turn, but she said that it was my boycott, nobody else minded the dishwasher being on. My sis thought this was a VERY good idea (I hate her, the brat). On Tuesday, everyone got microwaved vegetable lasagne and I got a *boiled egg. Next day I found my dirty clothes still in the linen basket. I asked Mum why and she said that I wouldn't want them being washed and dried in machines from Japan, would I? I hadn't thought of that so I said no and washed them myself in the sink and hung them out to dry. Unfortunately it rained all day so I had no clean socks on Thursday. I had to go round to the laundrette to use the dryer there. Mum said wasn't that Japanese as well and I said I didn't know and I didn't care. She just gave a nasty grin.*

But despite the attempts to make me give up the boycott, I am still sticking to it. I will not bow to pressure, but continue the struggle. I now know how people like Gandhi and Nelson Mandela must have felt. But I am not going to give in. Like the words of the song say:

I will not, I will not be moved, I will not, I will not be moved.

Love,

Sammy (leader of the BOYCOTT JAPANESE GOODS NOW! movement)

PS Do you want to support my boycott of Japanese goods?

PPS See – I really didn't mention Giles again, did I?

Dear Camille,

Well I didn't know you are going out with anyone called Tashimoto and you "certainly aren't going to boycott him" as you wrote in your letter. I suppose that this campaign is going to be a hard and lonely one, but nevertheless I am DETERMINED to continue my boycott. I will NOT be moved!

Love,

Sammy

Dear Camille,

*I've broken my boycott. I know what you're
going to say, as everyone else has said it
already. I couldn't stand any more. Jane's
cassette player chewed up three of my tapes,
including MULTI MEGA SWEAT HITS 7. My
hands look like monkey paws from all the
washing-up I've been doing and Dad wouldn't
take me anywhere in his car. The final
catastrophe was when Jane's parents bought a
satellite dish so I couldn't even find out what
was happening in Brookside. I will certainly
make sure that I persuade M and D to replace
anything that breaks down with non-Japanese
products. Although Dad said, when was the
last time you heard of Japanese goods breaking
down. He also pointed out the fact that if I
didn't watch any TV, I wouldn't be able to
check up on what the Japanese were getting
up to anyway – a good point, I thought (one
of his better ones). I was pleased at being able
to listen to CRAP RAP 3 on my Walkman
again.*

*Everything else is pretty boring at the
moment. I must admit, despite what I said*

about Giles, I am missing him – I think I'll
have to do something special for Valentine's
Day. Talking of hunks, I'm sorry to hear the
bad news about Tashimoto. I do feel that you
are right to tell him to get lost. Fancy having
the nerve to ask you round to his house for
some sushi! (and in front of your grandma). I'm
glad you told him where to go. Must go, Dad is
moaning about something as per usual.

Love,

Sammy

Dear Camille,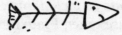

I think you made a bit of a mistake with
Tashimoto. Sushi is raw fish, not what we
thought it was, so I don't think he was being
rude at all. (Mind you, eating raw fish sounds
pretty disgusting!) And did he really try hari
kari when you gave him the boot? Never mind,
Giorgio sounds gorgeous – or do I mean
Giorgious? Of course, I'm not even looking at
other boys now I've got dishy hunky Giles.
YES – AGAIN!!!!

Valentine's Day worked brilliantly! I sent
Giles a card with the message "Someone thinks
you're wonderful". Then I wrote: "Meet me
outside MacWimpeys today at 4 o'clock and
bring a present for me." (I thought by putting
MacWimpeys, he'd never think it was me.)

On Valentine's Day, I got up dead early and
went to Giles's farm to make sure that the card
got delivered. I put it through the letter box and
zoomed off before anyone could see me. School
seemed to go on forever that day. Everyone
was talking about the Valentine cards they'd
got. Carol got a MEGA one – when she opened
it, it played the theme from "Love Story".

Classy hey?! Mind you, she just sneered and said something like "Won't he stop bugging me?" I got one as well! I think it was from Giles, because when I saw him later he looked embarrassed when I mentioned it. I think the only person not to get one was Hemmings! I took great delight in pointing this out to him when he asked me if I'd got a card and did I like it. (Hemmings being nosey again!)

When school was finished I got to MacWimpeys mega quickly and waited for Giles. He turned up right on time! I hid in the doorway of MacWimpeys and waited until he'd got his back turned. Then I moved behind him and put my hands over his eyes and in a sexy disguised voice said: "Hello Giles, this is your admirer. Have you got a present for me?" He nodded yes and seemed dead excited. I told him to close his eyes and turn round. As he did, I gave him a smacking great kiss! He said "Wow!" and then opened his eyes. I'm not sure how to describe what his face looked like as he realised it was me. He sort of gasped and his mouth went a bit like a goldfish. All he could say was "You!" I nodded. Just then there was a great cheering from the other side of the road - and cries of "Yo, Giles, go for it." It seems that his mates from the High School were all

98

watching. He went red (he's such a shy person), grabbed hold of me and pushed me into MacWimpeys.

Then we got chatting – he asked about what cards people had got, like Carol for instance. I told him about her card and what her reaction had been. Giles didn't speak for some time so I said that I forgave him for everything and I was sorry about the lights, but could we start again and before he could answer I gave him another kiss. There was another cheer because his mates had all crept in and were sitting opposite us. Giles went red again and said all right, as long as I didn't kiss him in front of his mates. Then he grabbed me and went outside to the cheers of his friends.

So, the romance is ON again. WHAM! has been abandoned and life is mega brill!

Love,

Sammy (back in L.O.V.E.)

PS How many cards did you get? – as if I should ask!

PPS In all the excitement, Giles forgot to give me the present.

Dear Camille,

*Has your postman recovered from his bad
back after delivering your Valentine's Day
cards? I was sorry to hear about Giorgio's
reaction to all the ones you got – but according
to Auntie Marge on "Teentalk Helpline", Latin
types are incredibly jealous in love. Talking of
which, Giles and I are still seeing each other
although I think there could be a bit of a cloud
on the horizon. It started at Earth Friends.
Michael Hemmings came to the last meeting
(can you believe it) and brought up the
question of fox-hunting. A fairly heated debate
followed, I can tell you. It ended with us all
saying that anyone who went fox-hunting was
demented. At the end of the meeting,
Hemmings came up to me and said I was a
hypocrite and why was I seeing a "demented"
person. Of course, I realised who he meant and
just went red. That night I rang Giles and
asked him did he ever go fox-hunting with his
dad? He said of course, he went riding with the
hunt every weekend. I started to tell him about
how bad it was, but he just went all superior
and said if I had never been to a hunt, how did*

I know what it's all about? This was a
ridiculous thing to say, of course, but I couldn't
think of a good reply, so I thought I'd better
find out more about it before tackling him
again about it.

Next day at school, I asked Boothie about
fox-hunting and he said that if I wanted to find
out more about it then I should go to a meeting
of the Anti Blood Sports Alliance. There's a
meeting next week, so I'm going to go and find
out the REAL facts. I haven't told Giles that I'm
going yet – better to keep this quiet until I've
been. I'll let you know what happens in my
next letter.

Love,

Sammy

February 24th

Dear Camille,

   To be honest, I'm glad Giorgio's girlfriend came over; I reckon you've had a lucky escape. Men are nothing but trouble, I don't know why we bother with them.

   I've felt sick all day, and just at the moment I could murder Giles. I went to the Anti Blood Sports Alliance meeting last night, and the things they told me about fox-hunting would make your hair curl – I know your hair is curly anyway, but you know what I mean. I've never liked the idea of fox-hunting, but farmers say they're a pest and if they weren't hunted they'd have to shoot them. But I reckon if you offered me the choice of being shot or being torn to bits by loads of slobbering blood-crazed hounds while a bunch of chinless pillocks sat around on horses going fwaw-fwaw-fwaw, I wouldn't need to think too hard about it. I bet even farmers get fed up with having their crops ridden over, and the people at ABSA told me that last year, a pack of hounds from one hunt ripped a kid's pet cat to bits in front of her. Apparently they couldn't tell the difference between a ginger tom and a fox; they must be

102

Fox

as stupid as their owners.

They don't even play fair! Before a hunt they send people out with spades to look for fox-holes and fill in as many as they can find, so the fox has nowhere to run to. And they call it SPORT! Then there's "cubbing". The hunts deny this goes on, but ABSA claim it's still happening though it was supposed to have been stopped yonks ago. What they do is, they find an earth and dig up the fox cubs. Then, because the hounds are so totally clueless they don't even know what they're supposed to be chasing, they chuck the cubs to them to be pulled to bits to give them the general idea. It's DISGUSTING!

It's a wonder any fox escapes, and I reckon it says a lot for the stupidity of fox-hunters that most of them do. That doesn't mean it isn't barbaric. There's a protest group going to the next meet on Saturday, and I'm CERTAINLY going to be there, no matter what Giles Wilson-Crawley says or thinks about it!

Love,

Sammy (militant)

PS I thought it best not to tell Giles that I'd been to the meeting.

Dear Camille,
    I'm never going to speak to Jane again!
She's dropped me in the you-know-what right
up to my eyebrows, I don't know what to do.
It's a good job there isn't a canal in this town
because if there was I'd throw myself in it.
    Do you know what she did? I asked her on
Tuesday (the day after the ABSA meeting) to
come on the anti-hunt demo with me (not that
I needed anybody to go with really, it's just the
more people there are on a demo, the better, for
publicity, you know). Anyway, she said she
wasn't sure, she'd think about it, so I left it at
that. Then on Wednesday I saw Giles. He was
in a foul mood – normally he's pretty docile,
he doesn't go in for great big hugs and kisses
to show how pleased he is to see me (worse
luck – it's just that he's shy I suppose), but
this time he was barely civil. I decided to do a
bit of probing to find out what the problem
was, but I didn't need to – he suddenly started
ranting about dumb idiots interfering with
things they knew nothing about. It seems his
mates in the hunt had heard about the demo
on Saturday and they were all totally furious

about it. I started to wonder whether going on a demo was such a good idea. I decided to see how he'd react by asking whether the people who were protesting against fox-hunting hadn't got a point. He glared at me as if I'd gone off my head and then he started going bananas. He said that people who protested against fox-hunting were long haired loony lefties with persecution mania (I think) who went about tormenting innocent hounds and spoiling people's legitimate enjoyment (obviously he'd got that lot off his dad); he went on to say that if he found anybody he knew (his eyes gave me a blast of X-rays at this point) mixed up in anything like that, he would "Know What To Do About It". I went all cold and changed the subject, but he wasn't really listening and after a bit he said he'd better go home. I asked him brightly whether he was going to finish cataloguing his butterfly collection, and he replied coldly that he wasn't doing much of that these days. I said he'd promised to get on with it, and one thing led to another, and we ended up having a tiff, if you can use that word for an argument that drowned out the traffic on the by-pass. I was too upset to go home, so I walked round for a bit, and later on I saw him talking to Zoe.

I decided then and there that I wasn't going to risk losing Giles over some stupid fox that couldn't look after itself. Maybe he was right, after all it IS traditional, and traditions ARE important, aren't they, I mean where would we be without morris dancing? So on Thursday I went to school determined that I wouldn't go on the demo. Michael Hemmings met me at the gate grinning like a gargoyle, which is always bad news. He started his stupid hound baying as soon as he saw me. I ignored him, of course, but when Michael Hemmings gets going, it's impossible to ignore him. He said he'd heard I was going on the anti-hunt demo. Jane had told him – can you believe it? She told me later she thought I'd wanted to find more people. I said people, yes; since when did Michael Hemmings qualify as people? She went all grumpy and said she'd only been trying to help. I suggested that next time she tried to help me, she could try eating a cement sandwich. This seemed to upset her, for some reason, so we're not speaking again.

Anyway I said that I'd decided not to go. Zoe and Carol ever-so-casually drifted by as Michael Hemmings's grin got wider and his eyes started to gleam until he looked like a Hallowe'en pumpkin. He said that was a pity as he'd told

everybody I was going; he'd even got his uncle (who works for local radio) to agree to do an interview with me, so I'd have a chance to put my views on the environment. I said I'd changed my mind about going, it wasn't really a major environmental issue, not like the rainforests, I was going to spend the weekend writing protest letters to double-glazing companies about using hardwoods instead ... Zoe started chanting chicken and Carol joined in, with Pig Hemmings grinning away in the background. Zoe sneered that I wasn't going because I knew Giles would finish with me if I went, and Carol said if I was chickening out just so as not to upset a boy it just proved I wasn't really serious about conservation.

I played it dumb and pretended not to know who they were talking about, and when Zoe mentioned Giles, I said, "Oh, will he be there?" dead casual like, but I don't think I fooled them. Zoe chanted chicken again and Carol said if I didn't go, they'd know what my concern for the environment was worth; Warthog Hemmings said so would everyone who listened to local radio, and he'd get the whole class to listen in specially.

    Just a minute – there's the phone.

    Ten minutes later.

That was Giles – he's just invited me to the Hunt Ball, which was nice of him; though he needn't have mentioned that he was only asking me because he was supposed to be going with Fiona Buster-Gussett or somebody, but she'd fallen off her horse and broken her leg. (I resisted the temptation to say I did hope she wouldn't have to be shot.)

So here I am on the Horns of a Dilemma – if I go on the demo, Giles will chuck me, and if I don't, I'll never be able to hold my head up again.

Have got to go now to post this. There's always the hope that I'll dream up a solution, or, better still, die in my sleep.

Love,

Sammy (agonised)

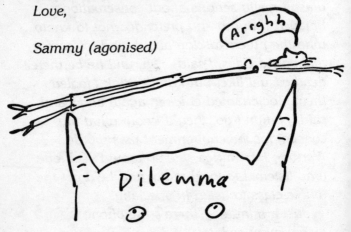

High Fever

Dear Camille,

Some people say things always look better in the morning. This is total rubbish! When I woke up on the morning of the hunt demo, I felt like death warmed up. Unfortunately, I obviously didn't look like it. As I staggered down to breakfast, Mum said that it was nice to see the roses in my cheeks. Typical − I said that it wasn't roses, it was high fever and I didn't feel at all well; she said nonsense, I was perfectly fit, anyway a day in the open air would do me the world of good. This remark caught me on the hop; she'd spent all week muttering on that demos were a waste of time and why did I have to go looking for trouble? I reminded her of this, and she said she'd decided as I was going to be out anyway she was going to do a major tidy around the house, and she certainly wasn't going to have me lying around making the place untidy. Again, typical − if I was on my deathbed she'd turn me out of it so she could change the sheets. I decided there was no point in pretending to be ill if she wasn't going to back me up − Sis would certainly spread it around that I was shamming. Why is it I can never get ill when I want to be? (I think I'll call this Sammy's Law: "No matter what a total sicko you are, you will always be perfectly fit on the day of a Maths test.") It certainly seemed unlikely I'd be struck down with bubonic plague in the next two hours. I began to feel sorry I didn't drink, smoke or eat meat, so that I couldn't even hope for a heart attack.

Then I had an inspiration! There were bound to be loads of people on the demo, there was bound to be a lot of confusion (that was supposed to be the point, after all). Giles probably wouldn't even notice I was there, especially if I went in DISGUISE!

Mum was enjoying herself trying to stop the hoover swallowing the curtains, so I slipped out and pinched one of her coats with the sort of collar that keeps your ears warm. I had a rummage in the bottom of Dad's wardrobe and found the scarf he used to wear when he was pretending to be Dr Who: I wrapped it round my neck and mouth so I couldn't be recognised. Just to be sure, I put on Dad's fishing hat and a pair of Sis's mirror shades.

I got some funny looks on the bus, but I wasn't bothered, especially after Maria Hicks from my class at school got on and sat down right beside me without recognising me!

When I got to the demo, I found the bloke I'd been talking to at the ABSA meeting. I stood around him for ages, but he kept looking away. Eventually I managed to grab his sleeve and go "Psssst." He glared at me, and I tipped back my hat and pulled the shades down my nose. He squinted.

"Oh, it's you," he said. "What in God's name are you dressed like that for? I thought you were bloody Special Branch or something." I said I'd decided to come incognito. He said never mind what I'd come in, it wasn't fancy dress, was I here to demonstrate or not? I said I was so he shoved a placard in my hand, and gave me a packet. He told me to throw it at the dogs and went to sort out the loud-hailer. I spotted Michael Hemmings's uncle fiddling with his tape recorder – I thought I'd wait until the hunt had set off, then go and introduce myself. If my class were listening in, I'd give them an earful!

There were quite a few of the hunt there, trying not to fall off their horses, shouting at the dogs and giving the demonstrators dirty looks. My heart stopped a bit when I saw Giles, and I pulled my head into the scarf a bit like a tortoise. I wondered which of the riders was his dad. Then the loud-hailer gave a screech, and the chanting started.

I soon got into it – it's dead exciting, feeling part of something like that, I can see why people go to football matches. One of the hunters rode over and started shouting something I couldn't hear. His horse nudged one of the protesters and when another grabbed its bridle the hunter (I found out later it was Giles's dad) tried to hit him with his riding crop.

Before long, there was a mob of horses, riders, demonstrators and dogs all over the place. One of the dogs bit somebody, which added to the confusion. I lost my placard, and found myself in the middle of the pack. I saw the bloke from ABSA waving at me and making frantic throwing motions with his other hand; I remembered the packet which I still had in my hand. Just as I wound my arm back to chuck it, a horse nudged me in the back, spinning me round. I found myself face-to-face with the horse. I couldn't stop the movement of my arm, and the packet burst right under the horse's nostrils.

For a second it just looked surprised; then it must have breathed in, and sniffed up a good bit of the pepper from the packet. Its eyes

bulged and it reared up on its hind legs.
The rider fell out of the saddle and snatched at
me as he went by, grabbing the end of my
scarf. I found myself spinning like a top; my
hat flew one way, my shades the other, and I
ended up lying on top of the fallen rider, who
was screaming at me to get off. I scrambled up
and was about to tell him what I thought of
people who couldn't control their horses when I
realised it was Giles. "You!" he boggled.
I thought quickly. "Excusez-moi, Senor,"
I babbled, "Ich bin une foreign exchange
student ..."

It was pretty weak. "You maniac!" he yelled,
turning purple. "Look what ..." He stopped, put
his hand to his shoulder, and winced and said
something about how I'd broken his collar
bone and crippled him for life. Then he lay
back and just moaned and groaned in a sort of
"oooowwwww" way. Something made me
say, "I suppose the Hunt Ball's off then, is it?"
(_STUPID_ COMMENT!)

He dragged himself up onto his good arm
and swore at me for yonks without repeating
himself once, until a couple of St John's girls
dragged him off to the tent. I felt gutted.

The rest of the hunt had gone by now, and
the protesters were getting into cars to harry

them, except for a couple the police had nabbed.

Then Michael Hemmings's uncle came over with his microphone. He asked me if I was Sammy. I just nodded and then he asked me to tell him in my own words what had happened this afternoon. I said, "I threw pepper at my boyfriend's horse, and he fell off it and broke his collarbone, and he's chucked me," and I burst into tears.

It went out on the six o'clock news.

I haven't seen Giles since. I sent some flowers to the hospital but they came back with all the heads pulled off. I sent a box of chocolates. Zoe produced them in break next day; she said Giles couldn't eat them as they would make him sick, so he'd asked her to share them round the class. She asked if I wanted one.

Dad's been getting at me too, he says Wilson-Crawley senior has been making his life more miserable than ever recently, had I done anything to annoy him? I said I hadn't, but I can tell he's still suspicious.

Still, who cares? At least I'll have more time for my campaigns on the environment now, I certainly don't need Giles, Zoe's welcome to him!

Love,

Sammy

PS Sorry about the wet blotches on the letter, Mum's been spraying the plants where I'm writing, and they must have dripped a bit.

PPS I have re-formed WHAM! (again).

Dear Camille,

Sorry I haven't written for ages, but thanks for your last letter. It made me feel much better after the G W-C affair (I refuse to write his name). And you're dead right; males ARE weak, pathetic creatures and not to be worried over or bothered about and we females are better off on our own. (Mind you, if you think this, why have you always got at least one boyfriend on the go?) Anyway, I have spent the last couple of weeks forgetting G W-C and devoting myself to Earth Friends and to saving the planet. We've organised a couple of things – a week away on an organic farm at Easter (when it's my <u>BIRTHDAY</u>, hint, hint). They don't use any chemicals on the farm and the only animals they have are cows that they milk – no destroying animals for the flesh eaters! We'll be helping to run the farm and grow things and also help to clean out a local canal – it sounds brill! M and D have said that they'll pay for it as my birthday present so it's worked out just right. Also, Mr Booth has organised a special guest speaker. Jonathon Porridge is coming to speak to us: he knows

EVERYTHING about the environment so he'll be great to listen to and also, he is a real HUNK! I've seen him on the telly. Mmmm!

In geography, we've been discussing the problems of the increase in the world's population. It's pretty scary because there's just too many people being born! I have therefore decided against getting married and having children. Michael Hemmings said that no one would want to marry me anyway, but I put that down to him trying to get his own back after an incident last week. Last Wednesday break, Hemmings came up to me while I was waiting to play ping-pong and asked me what I was doing on Friday! I looked at him as if he was something I'd found crawling in my salad and asked him why should he be interested, he wasn't by any chance asking me out was he? He went all red and shuffled his feet and said, well, er ... yes, but Alan Samuels asked him to do it for him. (Aren't boys pathetic having to get someone else to ask people out!) I suppose yukky Samuels had heard about G W-C and me splitting and reckoned he could get me on the rebound. I told Hemmings that if I did want to go out with a person of the male persuasion, Alan Samuels would be the last boy in the universe who I would want to go *out with. Then I thought about this a bit more and said no, sorry, I was wrong. Alan Samuels would be the SECOND-last person in the universe I would ever go out with. Hemmings asked me would the last person be G W-C by any chance and I said "No, Michael, it would be you." (Actually, he was right, it would be G W-C.)*

Just then, Alan Samuels himself wandered past looking gormless as usual. I was furious that he'd got Hemmings to do his dirty work, so I stopped him and pointed out in the nicest possible way that I was getting over a heartbreak, was the founder member of WHAM! and had no need of male company thank you very much, and if I did, I wouldn't choose someone who looked like a frog that had been run over. He looked at me as if I was mad, so I stormed off.

The weird thing is, it turned out later that Alan Samuels hadn't really asked me out at all! (Jane found this out when she came across Alan Samuels bashing Hemmings's head against the wall behind the bike sheds.) Jane reckoned Hemmings was really going to ask me out himself but then must have got cold feet. I reckon that Hemmings should be in some sort of home! Mind you, I felt a bit guilty when

I remembered what I'd said to him: you know how I feel about being kind to dumb animals. I wonder whether this rejection will cause him to kill himself? Ah well, we won't miss him, and it'd be one less head of population to worry about.

Love,

Sammy (Life President of WHAM!)

PS Your dad sounds almost as bad as mine. Fancy creating all that fuss when Jason came to the door, just because he had a Union Jack painted on his face – I thought parents approved of being patriotic.

Dear Camille,

Jonathon Porridge. Mmmmmmmm! What a hunko! He came to school to talk to us about how we can save the world by just doing little things. The hall was packed, but as a committee member of Earth Friends, I got to sit on the front row, right in front of him. He has got LOVELY GREEN eyes (very appropriate). Michael Hemmings was shown up as well! (He's been trying to get me back, ever since I made that "last boy in the universe" crack). He tried to organise a "support nuclear fuel and seal culling" protest. Adolf (the head) stopped him before he had a chance to start. Michael said he was doing it to bring political balance to the arguments. Adolf told him not to be so stupid and if he tried anything then he (Adolf) would start thinking about student culling, starting with anyone whose name was Hemmings! He was really shamed. Mind you I think Adolf was only concerned because there were a lot of press about and he didn't want the school getting a bad name. Hemmings went off muttering about fascism in schools – he is a nerd. Then he had the cheek to actually come to the meeting!

The talk was brill! Jonathon Porridge talked
for ages about what each of us could do for the
environment. Things like recycling and using
bottle banks, helping to stop acid rain by
switching off lights and using less energy, not
going to burger bars to stop rainforests being
destroyed, writing to people in power and all
things like that. I knew all about this (of
course) but it was good for the other un-green
people in the hall.

At the end of the talk he asked for questions.
I put my hand up and he looked straight at me
(I went a bit gooey!) and said "Go ahead".
I stood up and asked him if he thought that it
was a terrible thing to be building nuclear
reactors when things like Chernobyl happened
and how we can't get rid of nuclear waste and
if it was so safe then why didn't they have a
waste dump under the Houses of Parliament or
in the Prime Minister's garden and that
shouldn't we be spending money on renewable
forms of energy like sun, wave and wind
power, and then we could use the money we
saved to spend more money on saving the
rainforests by buying and eating more Brazil
nuts to save more trees, then the wildlife would
be better off and we could save hundreds of

species from distinction and cure acid rain as well? I think that this question certainly raised some new ideas for Jonathon because he looked puzzled for a minute before saying that it was an interesting question and I was probably right! HIM saying that to ME! I can tell you I sat down feeling VERY pleased. Michael Hemmings also put his hand up, and Jonathon asked him to put his question forward, but Adolf stared right at Hemmings so he said it was all right, he'd forgotten what he was going to ask. People giggled as he sat down – shamed TWICE in a day. Ha ha! So it was a brillo day for me. I think I will put Jonathon's ideas into effect right away.

Look forward to hearing from you soon.
Love,

Sammy (in love with JP!)

PS I am going to form a JP fan club. Do you want to join?

PPS WHAM! will now be called WHAM XJP! (We Hate All Men Except Jonathon Porridge).

PPS I am going to the organic farm next week (while we're there, it'll be my BIRTHDAY, hint,

*hint). Will write to you EVERY day, promise
(even on my BIRTHDAY!).*

April 21st

Dear Camille,

Here I am at the Back to Nature Organic
Farm. It's brill! As promised, I'll write to you
every day while I'm here (even on my
BIRTHDAY). We've just arrived and are settling
down. We're sleeping in tents, so that'll be
dead exciting – "sleeping under canvas, under
the stars and being close to nature". That's
what Boothie said. He also said how he
wished he could do it but unfortunately, he's
got to sleep in a boring bed in the farmhouse.
Quite a few of the class have come along:
Carol and Jane are here and so is Michael
Hemmings. Boothie announced last week that
there was a space left and Hemmings
immediately volunteered to fill it (don't know
why).

Anyway, this is going to be just a quick
note and I've put the address on, just in case
you want to send me a BIRTHDAY card or
BIRTHDAY present (as it's my BIRTHDAY on
Thursday).

The address is:
BACK TO NATURE ORGANIC FARM
SEEDLING, BEDS.

Look forward to hearing from you. I've got to go now as we're going to be shown how to milk a cow – fantastic!

Love,

Sammy

April 22nd

Dear Camille,

Well here I still am on the farm. It's been
very interesting so far although it's pretty tiring.
We were woken up at 4.30 am this morning –
by a cockerel! Jane said something about
wringing its b****y neck, but she was being
well grumpy – I thought it was brill and I
really felt close to nature being woken up as
the sun was rising. Breakfast was good – we
had some sort of crunchy muesli. Michael
Hemmings asked for bacon, black pudding and
sausages. The cook just looked at him.
Hemmings KNOWS it's a vegetarian farm and I
think he was just being awkward for the sake
of it. I said that he should eat the muesli as it
was good for him and he said it might be good
for him, but why did muesli always look and
taste like the droppings from a hamster cage?
Boothie said, "When was the last time you ate
hamster droppings, Michael?" Everyone
laughed and he shut up moaning. The milk we
had was from the cow we milked last night. It
was brill! We all had to go into the cow shed
where one of the farmers showed us how to sit
next to the cow and then squeeze the teats to

get the milk out into a bucket. We all had a go
and the farmer said I was the best at it and did
I want to have a go at milking later in the
week? I said yes, so I'm going to milk the cow
tomorrow – great, hey! (Mind you, it really
makes your hands ache.)

After breakfast we were told that we were
going to help fertilise the fields. Jane said that
she thought that the farm didn't use fertilisers,
but Dave, the farm manager, said yes it did,
but only natural ones and he'd take us to
where they were kept. He took us to the cow
sheds and gave us each a spade. Then he
pointed at all the cow-pats on the floor and
said, "There's the fertiliser, shovel it up, put it
in a bucket and carry it out to that field over
there." He pointed at a field that looked about a
mile away. Carol and Jane looked horrified at
this, but I smiled and said, "Come on,
everyone, let's get going, let's do it for the
environment," and started scooping up the pats
and putting them in the buckets. The first one
was dead easy, but after two hours' work of
filling the buckets, carrying them over a wall to
the field, then spreading it and digging it into
the soil, we were all shattered. Even Michael
Hemmings looked tired because after singing
"Old MacDonald had a Farm" (with some

words he must have picked up at the Rugby Club) solidly for twenty minutes, he shut up. Then it was time for lunch – we had a muesli and lentil bake which, to be honest, looked a little bit like the muesli we'd had for breakfast. (And tasted like it). I expected Michael Hemmings to say something, but even he was too tired to moan. After lunch we went down to the canal to start digging out the weeds. The laugh of the afternoon was when Jane fell in the canal and got covered in grey, gooey slime. She just stood in the middle of the canal, covered in this stuff, having hysterics! Mr Booth had to tell her to go back and have a shower. When we got back from clearing a bit of the canal, we found Jane still covered in slime because the showers weren't working. She was still having hysterics. We told Dave that the showers weren't working and he said he knew, in fact they hadn't been working for three months and we'd have to wash at the basin in the washroom. If this wasn't bad enough, we found out that there wasn't any hot water either. Still, as I said to Jane – you have to suffer for your beliefs if you're an environmentalist. I won't tell you what she said back to me.

Dinner was broccoli topped with muesli and

apple muesli crumble to follow. We're now all back at the tent, where I'm writing this by the light of my torch.

Yes, it's been a hard day, but I feel close to nature and the environment is certainly benefiting from my help!

Write to you tomorrow,
Love,

Sammy (at one with nature)

PS Nearly my birthday!

Dear Camille,

  I'm afraid that this letter is going to be fairly short as I'm shattered and my hands are aching so much that I can hardly hold the pen!

  The cockerel woke us up at 4.30 again. This time I agreed with Jane that it should have its neck wrung. Just as I was drifting back to sleep, the farmer came round the tents looking for me to milk the cows! I got up and staggered off to the milking sheds. I can honestly say I never ever want to milk 25 cows again ever. (In fact I never want to milk ONE ever again.) It took me until breakfast to milk them all. By the time I'd finished, my hands were aching so much, I couldn't hold my spoon to eat my muesli. Then it was fertilising the fields and then more muesli (with chick peas) and then canal clearing and then more muesli (with cheese) and now we're all back in the tent. The smell in here isn't too good – cold water washing doesn't go well with fertiliser spreading! Dave reckons that tomorrow will be a good day because the sky is red and the old country saying goes: "Red sky at night, Shepherd's delight". Hemmings muttered

something about "Sheep you can fry,
Shepherd's pie," which was pretty stupid, but
the idea of a yummy savoury mince topped off
with fluffy white mashed potato! It's a good job
I'm a vegetarian or I might have started
slobbering like Jane and Carol.

Got to go, as I'm falling asleep.
Love,

Sammy

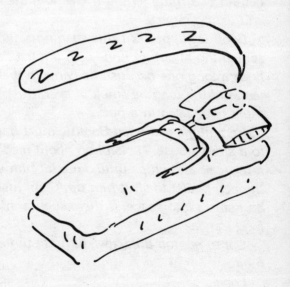

Dear Camille,

Never believe old country sayings. Or rather, make them up yourself. For instance: "Red sky at night; all night thunderstorms and tents getting flooded, all right!" We were soaked and flooded out.

Have spent the day trying to dry out between carrying fertiliser, cleaning the canal and eating muesli.

Boothie slipped out this evening saying something about a phone call. It must have been a long one because he came in well after tea, and the way he smelt of beer, the phone must have been in a pub.

Hemmings reckoned Boothie must have been to a steak house. He kept on about medium rare steak and chips until Jane hit him with the peg mallet to shut him up. Carol just sits and stares into space. Is there such a thing as a food trance?

Got to go, too tired/wet/filthy to write any more.

Love,

Sammy

PS At least it can't get any worse for my birthday tomorrow.

PPS Will write an extra long letter tomorrow to make up for this short one – honest!

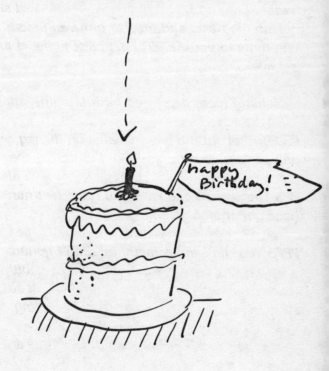

My Birthday, April 25th

Dear Camille,
    This has been the worst birthday I have ever had!
    I am too upset and tired to write any more. Will write to you AFTER I get back home.
    Love,

    Sammy (very depressed birthday girl)

PS Sorry about the brown stains on the paper – will explain everything when I write.

PPS The present and card you have sent me have not arrived yet.

PPPS You did send something, didn't you?

Dear Camille,

Sorry for not keeping my promise about writing to you every day at the farm, but when you hear about it you'll forgive me. I have just about recovered from the worst ever week of my life – the organic farm was more like a slave labour camp. We had to fertilise the fields and clear the canal every day. Even Boothie started to get annoyed with this, but he couldn't say anything because he'd suggested it in the first place. The food situation was so bad that I had a dream about eating a MacWimpeys and enjoying it! Aaghh! In fact, the last night we were there, I woke with a terrible pain in my leg and started screaming. I turned my torch on and found Carol biting my leg! She was blinking like an owl and obviously still half asleep. She said she'd been dreaming about eating roast leg of pork and must have tried to eat me! I've heard of sleep walking, but sleep eating??!!!

The water remained cold all week (except for the time it was FREEZING) and we stank of cow muck and rotting weeds. I smelt so bad that I had to spend two hours in the bath when

I got home and had to put my clothes through the washer 4 times before the brown, black and green stains came out of them. I was so pleased to get home that I gave my sis a hug, my dad a kiss and told my mum how much I loved her! That's how glad I was to be away from the organic prison.

Thanks for the birthday card and pressie – they were great. I got them when I got home (I thought you'd forgotten me when I didn't receive anything at the farm – which was strange because I think I mentioned my birthday in a letter to you).

My birthday was the worst ever! The cockerel woke us up at 4 and after a special birthday breakfast (two bowls of muesli), we started slopping out the cow-sheds again and carrying the stuff to the fields over the wall. Michael Hemmings, Jane and I were carrying a bucket each. We had a system for passing the buckets over the wall. When we got to the wall, I climbed over to the other side, Hemmings sat on the top of the wall, Jane passed the buckets up to him and he passed them down to me. The first bucket was passed without any trouble. Then it all went horribly wrong. As Jane passed Hemmings the second bucket, he looked in it and said, "Pheww, this

*is disgusting – it's all runny!" He took the
bucket from Jane and started to pass it to me,
telling me to be careful. Hemmings later
claimed that he slipped and it was a total
accident. All I can remember is reaching up for
the bucket and suddenly everything going
brown as the bucket, Hemmings and the cow
muck landed on top of my head. Pig
Hemmings was right for once – it was all
runny. I sat there covered in it, screaming my
head off. Jane looked over the wall and burst
out laughing and Hemmings just rolled around
the grass squawking with laughter. I started to
cry, then Jane said, "You have to suffer for
your beliefs if you're an environmentalist,
Sammy," and I swore at her.*

   *No one would come near me all day. I tried
to get as much of the stuff off as possible but
the cold water seemed to make it go like
wallpaper paste. Although the cook made me a
birthday cake (muesli and carrot) no one
wanted a piece after I'd cut it. Even Boothie
turned his nose up. So you now know why
there were stains on the letter you got and you
can guess what they were. The rest of the
week continued to be a nightmare and I was
very, very pleased when it was time to go
home. I am beginning to think that looking*

after the environment is beyond me – is it going to be this hard all the time? Ah well. As for organic farms – never again!

Love,

Sammy

PS M and D said I can come and stay with you in August (you're not thinking of moving to an organic farm are you?!).

PPS Give my regards to Raoul. When you say he does Flamenco dancing, are you talking about those big pink birds, or am I thinking of something else?

May 30th

Dear Camille,
 *HE'S LEAVING!! Mr Booth is LEAVING! I can't
tell you how awful I feel – he's only been here
a year. We were in registration today when he
said he'd got an announcement to make.
Hemmings said, "Oh God, not more green
stuff," and Boothie said, "No Michael,
something to make YOU happy."*

 *Boothie said he'd found teaching very
stimulating and a great challenge over the last
year and that was why he thought it was time
to go into something more restful and he'd got
a job selling double glazing. Pig Hemmings
cheered, of course, but I just sat there horrified.
Zoe made some crack about didn't the holidays
make teaching worth it, and Boothie said the
holidays were terrific, it was just the terms that
drove him round the bend. I said what about
Earth Friends and Boothie said since I was
about the only active member by now, he was
afraid it would be up to me to try and get
another member of staff interested – fat chance.
All they seem to be bothered about is saying
how fantastic the school is and writing stupid
publicity leaflets telling everyone that it's a*

139

great place (ha ha), so that everyone wants to come here. (Mind you, I bet all the other schools are doing the same so the biggest liars will get the most kids.) I seem to be wandering off the point. The point is NO ONE will run Earth Friends.

Anyway, after the rest had gone off to first lesson, I stayed behind to tell Boothie I was really sorry he was going – he seemed a bit surprised, so I said he'd really opened my eyes about the environment. He said, in a sarcastic sort of voice, that he thought I'd probably had enough of environmental issues to last me a bit. This made me think about all the things that had gone wrong since I joined Earth Friends but then I also thought about the importance of looking after the world and I remembered what Boothie had said about standing up for your beliefs. I felt really funny inside so I said to Boothie that I'd had a bit of trouble about being green, but after all, everybody had to learn didn't they, and it was all worth it really. He looked a bit thoughtful at that, and rummaged in his bag. He found some leaflets, and told me he'd not bothered, as he was leaving, to do anything about it, but there was a Walk for Whales in July and would I like to do it? I said I wasn't sure. I was still so *shocked about him saying that he's going.*

 He looked surprised at my answer and said well, think about it. At that point I felt my eyes filling with tears and had to run out of the room so he wouldn't see me crying.

 Have got to finish this now as I'm going to write to Auntie Marge at Teentalk Helpline.
 Love,

 Sammy (depressed)

Dear Camille,

Thanks for your letter. You're right! Although Mr Booth is a teacher, he is still a man and as you say, men will always let you down. Better advice than Auntie Marge, who said that I was being stupid and everyone has teachers who leave and I shouldn't worry because lots of people have teenage crushes on teachers! I mean, how stupid can you get! Me, a crush on Mr Booth?! Just because he's been a great help to me and made me realise how important the world is and I'm upset that he's leaving, some stupid woman has the nerve to say that I've got a "teenage crush"! I will NEVER listen to Auntie Marge on Teentalk Helpline again (AND I bet her name's not really Marge!).

Anyway, after reading your letter, I decided that just because HE's leaving doesn't make any difference to MY beliefs and ME standing up for them. So I told Boothie I would do the Walk for Whales. It's a sponsored walk, of course, to support the ban on whaling, so I thought I'd try to get more people to join in, but everyone seemed to have something else on that day. I was just telling Jane about it and

trying to persuade her to come when Michael
Hemmings came by, ears flapping as usual.
I ignored him, but instead of making some
stupid comment, he came over and said what
was all this about whales? I asked him if he
was interested in whales.

"Could be," he said.

Wonders will never cease! Jane wandered off
but I was too gobsmacked to notice. "You,
interested in whales?" I asked.

"Why not?" he said. "Is it south whales or
north whales?"

I'd never heard of those sorts of whales, so I
said I thought it was probably blue whales. He
looked puzzled, then said something about the
Preseli Mountains. I haven't a clue what he
meant by that and could have made some
comment about him never doing anything
green before, but nobody else was interested, so
I asked him if he fancied doing a sponsored
walk. He said he wasn't bothered about the
sponsored bit so I said leave all that to me, I'd
get sponsorship for both of us (I reckon the
whole world will give money if they think that
Michael Hemmings is going to do something
useful for once in his life). So off he went and I
stood there gobsmacked – Hemmings being
NICE for a change!

 143

So we're set to do the walk at the beginning of July – I must say, I'm quite looking forward to it.

Thanks again for the letter – and yes I am looking forward to coming to see you in August and meeting Raoul.

Love,

Sammy

PS I have put you down for £1 a mile – 50p for me and 50p for Hemmings. I can't believe he'll do the whole twenty miles, so you'll probably only have to pay me about £15.

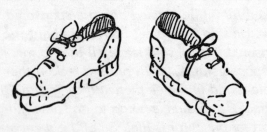

Dear Camille,

To be honest, I didn't think you'd be so snotty over a FEW pounds, especially as it's such a worthwhile cause. I have now crossed out the original amount and put you down for 5p a mile for me and nothing for Hemmings, like you said.

Sammy

PS And also I DIDN'T know that Raoul had been "cut from your emotional heartstrings for ever".

July 7th

Dear Camille,

I've got a feeling that this could be the longest letter EVER. I've got so much to tell you, and I can't wait until August to tell you in person, so you'll just have to find an hour when you can read this PROPERLY. (Good job it's written on recycled paper, otherwise a whole forest might have had to be cut down for THIS letter!) Right, I'm not sure where to begin. You're probably not going to believe a word of it anyway but it's all TRUE, even the bit about the sheep.

On the Sunday of the Whale Walk, I arrived at the coach dead early, just to make sure I was there before Michael Hemmings. To be honest, I didn't think he'd turn up. But he did and I couldn't believe it! I was just wearing jeans and trainers with an anorak of my dad's, but he had all the gear – walking boots, those legging things and a proper rucksack! I said something about it and he went all red and said, "Well, I do a lot of walking." Funny, isn't it, how you think you know all about somebody? Boothie was there of course, with a woolly hat and hairy trousers. He looked a bit

146

surprised to see me and Michael Hemmings together, but I couldn't be bothered explaining, so I just said, "Morning, sir" and left him to work it out for himself.

When we got on the coach I told Michael Hemmings about all the other green things I was doing. He must have had a late night on Saturday because he fell asleep almost at once and was still snoring when we reached the place where the walk was to start. He woke up when I reached for my bag off the luggage shelf and dropped my Thermos on his head.

The walk was started by a wildlife artist who looked like a sort of a bird's nest with legs, and he told us some really interesting things about whales, but I noticed Michael Hemmings wasn't listening. He was looking round in a puzzled sort of way. I went over to him and gave him his registration card, and he said, "This doesn't look like Wales." That's because it's Derbyshire, I told him. He looked mega shocked and said that I'd said Wales.

"Correct. Whales," I replied. "Big fish. Blubber, Porpoises, Dolphins, Moby Dick. Whales." He looked well annoyed and said that he thought he was coming for a walk in Wales.

I told him it served him right for eavesdropping and anyway it was a walk wasn't it? He calmed down, but kept on muttering "Derbyshire" under his breath as we followed the other walkers out of the car park.

After a bit he asked how long the walk was supposed to be. I told him it was twenty miles. He shrugged, and we went on. We walked for ages and my feet were beginning to hurt a bit so I asked Michael how far we'd come. He reckoned about three miles.
I looked at him gobsmacked. THREE MILES? I couldn't believe it! Only three miles, and we had to do twenty! I asked him if he was sure. He said he wasn't certain but he'd check it on the map and could I pass it to him.

"You said YOU had a map," I said.

He went a bit spare about that and shouted that he thought we were coming to Wales and how he'd got every map from Swansea to Prestatyn in his rucksack, but that wasn't going to help us in Derbyshire. He then asked me if I had a map.

"They'd run out," I told him. He went even more spare about that until I said it was his fault for being last off the bus. "Anyway," I said, "we can follow the others."

He pointed out that the others were so far ahead we couldn't see them thanks to me walking about as fast as a ruptured slug. I told *him it was his own fault for arguing too much. I also told him it didn't matter about a map because all we had to do was follow the markers. He started raving on about being properly prepared for walks with whistles and survival blankets and Bovril but I ignored him – there were big yellow arrows on gates and things showing the route, all we had to do was follow them.*

Then the mist came down.

I blame the organisers – don't they listen to weather forecasts? Anyway, as I told Michael Hemmings, I'd collected all the sponsors' names, the least he could've done was check the weather. "I did," he snarled, "for Wales. It's sunny in Wales." I told him he was getting boring on the subject of Wales, and mist wasn't seasonable for the time of year in Derbyshire (I don't know if that's true but I was fed up with him moaning). I was just about to tell him that the strange weather was all part of the break-up in the world weather systems caused by CFCs when I suddenly went up to my thighs in black evil-smelling mud. I was sinking! I shouted for help, and he just turned round and looked at me! If he'd been Indiana Jones, he would've flicked his whip around my arm, and pulled me to safety; as he was Michael

Hemmings, he kicked at a stone and asked
when I was going to stop messing about?

"I'm in a bog!" I screamed at him.

He kicked another stone. "It's not a bog," he
said, "it's only a peat hag. The moors are
covered in them – just pull yourself out."

I gaped at him.

"Get me out before I smash your head in!"
I yelled.

He grinned nastily and said that if he didn't
get me out then I wouldn't be able to smash
his head in. Then he added, "Anyway, what's
wrong with 'please'?"

I flipped! "PLEASE get me out before I smash
your head in!"

He sighed and took off his rucksack and
stretched out his hand to me.

I'm not sure what happened next but I
must've pulled before he was ready or
something, because I seem to remember him
doing a sort of loop-the-loop, and then he was
flat out in the mud beside me. He lifted his face
out of the mud and just stared at me. I burst
out laughing – I couldn't help it.

He spat out a few bits of peat and asked
what was so funny? After a few minutes to
catch my breath, I managed to gasp and ask
him if he knew what he had given me. "No," he

snarled, "what?"

"A dirty look!" I said. That set me off again.

For a moment he looked well mad. Then he looked at me and he started chuckling. We must've looked a right pair of loonies, caked in black mud, rolling about in a mud hole in the middle of Derbyshire roaring with laughter.

After a bit, Michael said we'd better get on and he helped me pull myself out, and got a towel from somewhere in his rucksack – it wasn't much use, but it did get some of the mud off.

Then we went on. I kept closer to him now – in fact, I sort of clung on to his arm – after all, I thought, there was no point in risking falling into another peat hag, was there?

About half an hour later, we came to a drystone wall. I hadn't a clue which way we should go but Michael said we should go left as the land seemed to slope down that way and on the moors, you were more likely to find houses and roads and things in the valleys where there were streams and shelter. That all seemed so sensible that I couldn't believe Michael Hemmings was saying it. We carried on and came across a barbed wire fence. After a discussion about whether it was a fence to keep people out or a fence to keep things in,

151

like a bull, we decided to climb over it. Michael went first and held the barbed wire down for me before setting off again. That's when I threw my arms around his waist. He gave me a shocked look and was about to say something when he saw the look on MY face.

"Look down," I said, "... but very, very carefully."

I suppose the mist must've been a sort of low cloud, because half a second before I pulled Michael back, it parted, and I saw what he saw when he turned his head. His toes were sticking out over a cliff. About a million miles below us there was an ugly green pool of water.

He licked his lips. "It's a quarry," he whispered. "Tell you what – let's step back a bit."

I asked him if I should let go of his waist and he said "no" and I said "right".

As I took one step back the ground crumbled under his feet. I let go of his waist and grabbed his rucksack. Then we had a competition to see who could scream loudest. I just held on to the rucksack and pulled, I was yelling nonsense, I don't know how I did it, but suddenly we were away from the edge and sort of hugging each other ...

I mean, of course, he was hugging me. I was sort of comforting him in a sisterly sort of way.

He said "Thanks" and I said that was okay and he said that if I hadn't hung onto his rucksack then ...

I looked at him and said that I had to. He asked why?

"'Cos it's got the sandwiches in it," I said.

It started to rain.

We went down the hill. We were holding hands – it seemed natural after what had just happened. The rain was really heavy now and Michael offered to lend me his waterproof, but I told him to keep it – after all, I was the one who came unprepared. He put it on but left the hood down, which seemed daft.

Ages and ages later we came to this building. It looked like a badly put up coal shed, but at least it seemed to have a roof, or most of a roof. There was a door with a string latch, so we went in. There was no window, but the door didn't fit well, and light came through holes in the roof; so did rain, but there were dry bits and some bales of straw. I just zonked out. Michael poked about a bit and said it was probably a place some farmer kept his sheep in when the weather was bad. I gave him a look.

"I mean really bad," he said, "like in winter when it's so cold the wind makes your eyes water and the tears freeze on your cheeks." I said I'd rather be in bed with a good book in weather like that, and he said that it was often the best weather for walking, when everything was clear and crisp and you could make fresh tracks through unbroken snow like Robinson Crusoe and feel you were the only human being alive. (I thought Robinson Crusoe made his footsteps in SAND but Michael was well away so I didn't interrupt him.) He told me about walking in the Lake District and Snowdonia. I suppose anywhere else I'd have found it all dead boring, but somehow, sitting in that broken down shack with rain dripping through the roof, I found myself listening and sort of imagining it all, what it would be like.

Then I must have dozed off. I woke up with a start to see Michael rummaging through his rucksack. I looked at my watch and discovered it was three o'clock. Great! – the coach would leave at five and where would we be then? I must have asked this aloud because he said, "About where we are now, I should think," and passed me a sandwich. I was halfway through before I realised what it was.

I spat a mouthful out. "It's liver sausage!"

He wasn't a bit bothered and said something about how he thought it was peanut butter.

I felt ill. "You've made me eat liver sausage!" I shouted at him. He didn't get it and said it wouldn't kill me.

"That's not the point, you boneheaded nerd," I shrieked. "It's meat! Some bloodsucking murderer had to kill a poor defenceless animal to get it ..."

He sighed and wrapped the packet up and muttered something about saving the rest for later. I sat and shivered at him. He listened to my teeth chattering for a bit and then asked me if I was cold. I gave him a what-kind-of-stupid-question-is-that? look.

He shuffled his feet and said that he'd got a sleeping bag in his rucksack. I gave him a don't-you-dare-even-think-about-what-I-think-you're-thinking look.

"I mean," he said hurriedly, "it's got a zip round two sides, it opens out dead big ..."

I suggested in the nicest possible way that if his idea was that we should share his rotten sleeping bag, I'd rather be dead in a ditch. He sighed and said I could have it.

I thought why not? After all, he was the one who had got us lost, he practically made me fall into that bog, I'd already saved his stupid

*life, then I looked at him and saw that he was
shivering, too. I thought about it. I said, "Back
to back?" He nodded, so I said okay then.*

*I must say, it was lovely and warm wrapped
up in his sleeping bag. I said it was a good
bag. He said it ought to be, it was down. I said,
"Down what?" and then I realised what he
meant. "You mean feathers?" I said. He said
yes. I sat up and asked him if they had to kill
the birds to get the feathers.*

*He groaned and said he hadn't the faintest
idea, perhaps they sheared them, like sheep.
I said you couldn't shear chickens, you
plucked them, and you could only do it when
they were dead because otherwise they tended
to object. He said they weren't chicken
feathers, they were duck feathers. I said what
difference did that make, and he said they
were better insulation. I said, no, I meant what
difference did it make whether it was ducks or
chickens that got killed, the point was ...*

*He said the point was, when was I going to
get off his back and stop picking on him all the
time?*

ME????? ! ! ! !

*I asked him what he thought he was
gibbering about. "Sammy," he said (that's the
first time he'd ever called me by my first*

name), "the trouble with you is, you don't know when to stop."

He asked me why I didn't talk about things normal girls talk about? What does "normal girls" mean? I thought and said, "Such as what?"

He thought a bit and then said that he didn't know, but things that Carol and Zoe talk about, like clothes and music and films and Neighbours and who's going out with who. I replied that I did talk about those things. He snapped back that I certainly did not because all I ever talked about was conservation this and the environment that. (Can you believe it??!!)

I told him that conservation and the environment are important. That stopped him and he had to agree with me. But then he added, "Important, but not all there is." I started to feel a bit peculiar, and asked him what did he think he was getting at?

He then said lots of "I means" and "what ifs" and "don't yous" before he finally blurted out, "What I mean to say is, don't you ever think about having a boyfriend?"

I thought about this and said, "Like Giles, you mean?"

"No, not like Giles," he replied and turned

his back on me, saying that I should forget that he'd said anything.

I lay there and thought about what he'd said. I suppose in a stupid way, he'd been trying to ask me out, and properly this time. Of course, I wouldn't ... but it was a sort of compliment, I supposed; I knew a few girls who wouldn't have minded going out with Michael. I didn't have time to mess about with boys of course, what with the G W-C incident and being the founder of WHAM! and all the campaigning I had to do, but if he wanted to help me with a few bits of it ... He wasn't really that bad-looking, and he could be quite nice when he wasn't talking rubbish or acting stupid ... I suppose some girls would even call him hunky. I drifted off and the next thing I knew, Michael Hemmings was kissing me passionately! I didn't know what to do! Of course, I should have belted him with a large rock, but – anyway, it was sort of nice, really, to be honest, being all warm and comfy and only half awake in the sleeping bag and having my face showered with burning kisses. He kissed my nose and I giggled.

"Don't be so soft, Michael," I said.

He said, "Mnnneeeeeeerrrrrrr."

I opened my eyes and sat bolt upright, and

the sheep that had been licking my face went pelting out of the open door in a panic. A SHEEP! Licking my face! I sat and mega cringed! Then looked around for Michael. He'd gone! I was petrified for a moment, but then I heard voices, and an engine start up, and he came running back in through the door, and grabbed his rucksack. "Come on," he yelled, tugging at the sleeping bag which I was clutching under my chin, "or they'll go without us."

"Who will?" I yelled back as he dragged the sleeping bag off me and went belting out again. I grabbed my own bag and went to the door. The mist had lifted a bit. About two hundred metres off down the hillside was the car park where the walk had started, and the coach was sitting there with all its lights ablaze, revving its engine.

At least Michael had the decency to stand in the doorway and wait for me, though I could have done without the "Come on, slowcoach!" he yelled as I climbed the wall (and the ironic cheer that came from the rest of the walkers in the bus made me feel well stupid). The driver looked at him, and then at me, as I staggered up the steps and asked, "What've you two been up to, then?" I replied that we'd got lost in

the mist.

He whistled through his teeth and said to Michael that he'd have to marry me now!

Of course, Boothie WOULD be sitting in the front seat. He started to make a horrible nasal noise – it took me a few seconds to realise he was laughing.

Honestly, adults can be so stupid at times.
Love,

Sammy

PS This has taken me ages to write and my arm's aching. I hope you appreciate the effort!

PPS You don't have to pay up your sponsor money as we didn't finish the walk!

PPPS Don't you dare tell ANYONE about anything in this letter!

17th July

Dear Camille,

Yippee! Last day of term was today! No more school for weeks! (plenty of homework though, worse luck).

At the final assembly today, Adolf, the head, announced that Boothie was going and made a speech all about what a terrific contribution he'd made to the life of the school, though personally I doubt whether he had the slightest idea who Boothie was or whether he'd done anything at all. Our class presented Boothie with a pen, which was the least we could do considering we'd nicked at least six of his during the year. Carol (the creep) asked Boothie what he'd miss most about teaching and he said that was difficult to answer but it was a choice between the sleepless nights and the constant insults. He said he would take a great deal of interest in our future careers and make a special point of watching Crimewatch UK to see how we were doing. He was joking, of course. At least, I think he was. Anyway, I was sorry to see him go, and I think most of the others were – even Michael Hemmings seemed pretty subdued, but I hadn't spoken to him since the Whale Walk (I think he's been avoiding me) so I didn't know whether he was sorry Boothie was going, or something else was bothering him.

We got let out half an hour early (wow, big deal!) so I thought I'd drop you a quick note – I'm really looking forward to seeing you in a couple of weeks. We can swap all the gossip and I'm really looking forward to meeting Dominic – if he's still around when I get there (joke ha-ha). There'll be such a lot to talk about, you can hardly put anything in a letter!

There's the doorbell – must go.

Love,

Sammy

PS – MUCH, MUCH later ...
You'll never guess who was at the door – Michael Hemmings! I was gobsmacked! He'd dressed really smartly, for once, with his shirt tail inside his jeans and clean trainers and everything – he looked much better out of school gear, nearly human!

He said, "Hi," and stood there on the step like a spare part. I didn't want the neighbours laughing so I asked him to come in. We went into the lounge and sat down. I said did he

want a coffee? He said, "No." I said "Tea?" He
said "No." I said "Coke?" He said "No."

I got fed up with doing all the talking so I
just sat and looked at him for a bit while his
eyes roamed about all over the room. Finally he
looked at me and said, "Nice".

I wasn't sure whether he meant the room or
me, but what with Mum's dodgy macrame,
Sis's stupid donkey from Torremolinos and
Dad's crossed swords over the fireplace, on a
good taste scale of 1-10 our lounge scores about
minus 1000 so I decided he meant me and
smiled at him.

It seemed to liven him up a bit. He started
talking about the Whale Walk. He said it was a
bit of a washout (understatement of the
century!).

"Thanks," I said and then he started getting
all flustered and started stammering! He said he
didn't mean it like that and that he'd enjoyed
bits of it – "like when ...". He shut up as I
gave him a 50,000 volt glare right between the
eyes; if he thought he was going to start going
on about what happened in that hut ...

"If you ever breathe to a living soul that I
shared a sleeping bag with you," I hinted, "I'll
superglue your mouth shut."

He looked shocked, and said, "I wouldn't do

that!" I said that I bet he'd boasted to all his mates about it already, but he swore on his life that he hadn't. So I told him that he'd better not.

He came over all huffy and said that he'd come round because of the sponsor money. I pointed out that we hadn't had any sponsor money because we never finished the walk.

Then he said yeah, but he'd gone to see the bloke in charge and had looked at the map and shown him where we'd gone, and they'd worked out that we must have done just over eight miles. I couldn't see what he was going on about. "So what?" I asked.

Michael smiled and said, "So he's signed our sponsor forms to say we've done that amount."

All I could do was shrug and wonder "So what?" again. Then Michael said that he'd gone round all the sponsors I'd got and collected it in. He said that it wasn't as much as we'd have got if we'd done the full distance, but that some people paid full whack anyway, so it wasn't far off the full amount. (You owe me 40p!)

"Here it is," he said and put one of those see-through plastic envelopes you get from banks, with money in it, on the coffee table.

I didn't know what to say. I wanted to

shrink and crawl down the side of the sofa cushion to hide until he'd gone. I felt myself going red, and went funny inside.

Then the MAJOR gobsmack bit ...

"And ...," he said, taking a deep breath, "I came to ask if you'd like to see a film tonight."

Someone with a voice like Minnie Mouse (and as there was no-one else in the house, it must have been me) asked what was on. He said that there was a film at the Odeon about a kid being brought up by a South American tribe in the rainforest.

We went to the Odeon. Michael had got the times wrong, and "The Emerald Forest" had already started, so we ended up going to see a western instead; but it didn't matter.

Love ....

Sammy

SON OF A GUN
Janet and Allan Ahlberg

A galloping, riotous wild west farce in which the plot thickens with every page until a combined force of Indians, US cavalry, old-timers, dancing-girls and the eight-year-old hero are racing to the rescue of a mother and baby, besieged in their cabin by two incompetent bandits called Slocum. As one of the Slocums says, 'Cavalry *and* Indians? Where's the fairness in that?' — *New Statesman*

HENRY AND RIBSY
Beverly Cleary

Henry's dream is to go fishing with his father. He can just see himself sitting in a boat, reeling in an enormous salmon. Mr Huggins has promised he will take Henry fishing on one condition: that he keeps Ribsy out of trouble and does not let him annoy the neighbours, especially Mr Grumble next door. The trouble is, keeping a dog like Ribsy under control isn't that easy!

CRUMMY MUMMY AND ME

Anne Fine

How would you feel if your mother had royal-blue hair and wore lavender fishnet tights? It's not easy for Minna being the only sensible one in the family, even though she's used to her mum's weird clothes and eccentric behaviour. But then the whole family are a bit unusual, and their exploits make very entertaining and enjoyable reading.

WILL THE REAL GERTRUDE HOLLINGS PLEASE STAND UP?

Sheila Greenwald

Gertrude is in a bad way. She's a bit slow at school, but everyone thinks she's dumb and her teachers call her 'learning disabled' behind her back. As if this isn't enough, her parents go off on a business trip leaving her with her aunt and uncle and her obnoxious cousin, Albert – a 'superachiever'. Gertrude is determined to win Perfect Prize-winning Albert's respect by whatever means it takes ...

TALES FROM THE SHOP THAT NEVER SHUTS
Martin Waddell

McGlone lives at the Shop that Never Shuts, and Flash and Buster Cook are in McGlone's Gang with wee Biddy O'Hare.

In these five highly entertaining stories the Gang dig for Viking treasure, are frightened that a sea monster has eaten Biddy, discover that McGlone needs glasses, look after the Shop that Never Shuts on their own, and give Biddy a birthday party.

VERA PRATT AND THE BALD HEAD
Brough Girling

When Wally Pratt and his fanatic mechanic mother enter the Motorbike and Sidecar Grand Prix, nothing is really as it seems. Vera's old enemy, Captain Smoothy-Smythe, is up to his old tricks and suddenly Wally is kidnapped. Rescue him? She can't do that yet, she's got to win the Grand Prix first. Two minutes to go and Vera finds herself the ideal partner – a headmaster with no hair!